After Summer

S R Silcox

Published by Juggernaut Books Pty Ltd

ISBN-13: 978-0-9924126-9-2

ISBN-10: 0-9924126-9-2

www.srsilcox.com

Second Edition

For my wife's sixteen-year-old self.

Five years ago...

The old shed shook with every crash of thunder and every flash of lightning. Riley huddled so close against me, I thought she was going to crawl into my skin. I pulled her tighter against me and stroked her hair, telling her it was going to be okay.

For me, this storm was nothing to be worried about. They came and went so quickly up here in the tropics, I was used to them. Riley only came up here for a few weeks in the summer, so she wasn't used to them being so ferocious.

The sky lit up, and a flash of lightning boomed somewhere close, shaking the ground and the shed with it. Riley whimpered and curled up tighter. I wrapped my arms around her and rested my chin on the top of her head. "It's okay, Rols. It'll be over soon, I promise."

Another boom of thunder. Riley shuddered.

"Brooks?" she whispered.

"Yeah?"

"If I die—"

I almost laughed. "You're not going to die, Roly," I said.

She picked at the friendship bracelet on my wrist. We'd given them to each other last summer. "If I die," Riley said, "you need to know something."

"What?"

Riley looked up at me and I could see the terror in her eyes. Our faces were so close, I could feel her breath on my skin. She whispered, "I love you, Brooks."

One

Riley

If you don't count Mum's funeral four months ago, today is the first time I've seen my dad in over five years. After my parents split up when I was three, he'd fly me up to Roper's Beach after Christmas every year for his access visits. When I was eleven, he started to get really busy with his company and got remarried. I guess after the first year he cancelled, it was easier to just not come up anymore.

By the time I fly into the airport in Townsville, it's seven at night. I had a six hour delay in Brisbane thanks to storms rolling through up here in the north, and even though this last flight was only two hours, I'm so tired, I can't even really feign the excitement I should probably show when I see Dad standing at the arrivals gate.

He looks as dishevelled as I feel. When I was a kid he used to pick me up in board shorts and thongs. Now he's standing in front of me in a crumpled business shirt and dark jeans. He rushes over to grab my bags from me and gives me an awkward hug.

"Sorry the flights were a pain," he says. "Storm season's started early up here." I shrug in response. He hoists a bag over each shoulder, and as he leads me out of the terminal he says, "Trip home'll take longer than usual. Julie called and said there are some trees down on the road in. Should be cleared by time we hit the turn off though."

We get to Dad's car, (a convertible of some sort, which is a huge upgrade from the surfie van he used to drive), and my legs are starting to feel like lead. I can feel my body fighting off sleep. Dad throws my bags in the boot and when he goes to take my backpack, I pull it away from him. "I'll hold onto it." He doesn't question me, and as I sit in the passenger seat he says, "Put your seat back and have a sleep. I'll wake you up when we get there."

I tuck my pillow between my head and the window and as we head out of the car park, I close my eyes and drift off.

Dad woke me as we got to the turn-off, just like he used to if I'd fallen asleep in the car on the way in, but all he's said to me since then is, "I hope you like the new place. It's a lot bigger than the old shack." I think I grunted in reply. I liked the old house Dad used to live in up here, but I guess when you have a new wife and a step-son, you need something bigger than a two-bedroom shack to live in.

It's around ten by the time we turn onto the esplanade at Roper's Beach. It's also raining, which means I don't get to see the water as we drive along the foreshore. When I used to come here, if I got in at night, the moon would reflect off the water like a spotlight and I'd be able to see the silhouette of the island, but tonight it's dark and miserable.

I look past Dad and out his window at the houses as we drive along. The speed limit on the esplanade has always been slow, so I get a chance to take in what I can see through the rain and the orange street lights. There are big new double-story houses that look like fortresses behind their tall fences in amongst some older weatherboard ones. It's funny how the old places never seem to have fences but the new ones do. Dad probably built the newer ones.

We drive past the little shopping strip that's been here since before I was born and I'm happy to see that the Burger Hut is still there. It looks like it's expanded on the side, but apart from that, the sign with the hot dog eating a burger from one hand and holding a milkshake in the other still stands proudly on the roof. I'm not sure why, but seeing that hot dog man makes me feel a little better about being up here.

"Gloria and Stav still own it," Dad says as we cruise past. "They just got some new pizza ovens, so that'll be a nice change. We won't have to go into town to grab a pizza anymore." I don't say anything in reply, but continue watching as we drive along the road.

We drive past a couple of vacant blocks of land and then the caravan park comes into view. The few times Mum came up with me for holidays, we'd stay there instead of at Dad's. The wooden palm tree with the missing branch that Brooks Doherty and I broke when we tried to climb up the side of it is still out the front, lit up by a spotlight. There's a sign tacked onto it that says 'Bait sold here' but the one that catches my attention is the one that says in bright red letters on a white background 'Under New Management'. That one throws me a little because it used to be run by Brooks' Uncle Pete and if Pete's not here anymore, then there's a good chance Brooks will be gone too. She always said she'd be getting out first chance she got.

"Isn't Pete here anymore?" I ask.

Dad looks a little surprised by my question, but that's probably because I've hardly spoken to him the whole trip. "He's on holidays," he replies. "Sold his share back to the other owner and they got a semi-retired couple in for a couple of months until they can find someone more permanent."

"Oh." I turn back around in my seat to look out at the blackness that would normally be the beach.

Dad slows down and turns into a long driveway. "Here we are," he says. We pull up in front of a double-bay garage and wait for the automatic door to open.

We park beside Dad's work trailer, 'Scott Fisher - Builder' emblazoned on the side. It doesn't look like it's been moved in a while, judging by the deflated tyres.

There are surf boards and mountain bikes stored above it on the ceiling and the whole place is so neat and tidy, I have to wonder whether Dad is even a builder anymore. Maybe being married again makes him more organised. Or maybe Julie's the neat one?

Dad carries my bags for me, and I follow him around the back of the house where he leads me past the pool down to what looks like a tiny house. "I've put you in the guest house. Thought you might like your own space." Dad slides open the glass door and turns on the inside light. "It's all fully self-contained, so you've got your own shower and everything. Kitchen too, if you want to do your own cooking."

He looks proud of himself, so I fake a smile. I can't believe he doesn't want me in the main house but I'm too tired to argue right now. He drops my bags in the middle of the floor and after digging around in his pockets, produces some keys. He hands them to me. "These are your set for here and the house. You can come and go as you want over the holidays and after you're settled in we'll discuss house rules. Did you want to come up and have something to eat?"

I shake my head. "I'm good. I think I'll just have a shower and go to bed."

Dad nods. "Okay then." He takes a step back towards the door and then stops. "Oh, before I forget. I called the moving company today, and they should have your boxes and things up here sometime over the weekend. So, anything you need, just ask."

"Thanks," I reply.

"Tomorrow morning, just come up when you're ready and Julie will get you some breakfast. Or whatever," he says. "And um." He waves in the general direction of the guest house. "Just make yourself at home."

"Okay."

He taps his hand on the door and gives me a quick smile. "I'll see you tomorrow then. Goodnight, Riles."

"Night, Dad."

I take a moment to check out the guest house. It's basically one big L-shaped room, with a bed in one part, a small lounge under a window in front of the bed, and where I'm standing near the door, a kitchen sink and a round wooden table with four chairs. There's a door off to the side of where the bed is which I assume is the bathroom. At least I won't have to share a bathroom with my step-brother, Jason.

I put my backpack onto the table, open it up and take out Mum's wooden ashes box. After the long day I've had, it feels heavy in my hands. I trace the laser-cut rose on the top of it with my fingers, the design she picked out herself, and sigh. If she'd been able to hold on for just one more year, I wouldn't have had to come back up here. I shake my head to get rid of that thought, because of course Mum had no say in when she died.

I look around for somewhere to put the box and settle on the bench by the window, which has a view of the pool outside. Mum always said she wanted a room with a view.

I stand for a moment and look out the window where the rain has finally stopped and the yard is lit up by the blue lights from the pool. I wish I didn't have to be here, but there's nowhere else I can go. I touch Mum's ashes box one more time and head over to my suitcase to find my pyjamas. I don't want to think about the fact that the rest of my so-called new family is in the other house right now. I just need some sleep.

Two

Brooks

I eye the yellow envelope sitting on the kitchen bench. So far, I've resisted opening it. Yesterday, it was sitting on the table in the hall where we put all the mail but Ben must have gotten tired of me ignoring it and put it where I have to look at it. It's addressed to my parents' house, so either Mum or Dad would've dropped it off here, and I can tell by the way the flap on the back is all mangled that someone, most probably my mother, has already opened it. That would explain why she wants to talk to me again all of a sudden.

There's a weight of expectation inside that envelope and I'm not sure I'm ready to see whether it's good or bad just yet. Ben appears in the kitchen, a towel around his waist, his hair still dripping wet after his shower. "I wish you wouldn't eat those," he says, referring to my late night snack of Coco Pops. He opens a cupboard and pulls out his shake mix.

"Like you can talk." I tip up the bowl to get the last of the chocolate milk from the bottom.

"This is much healthier than some of the stuff you put in your mouth," he says, measuring out the powder into his shaker.

"At least mine's made from real food and not in some lab."

He snorts.

"What?" I ask.

"That is not real food. And it's not good for you." Ben shakes his dinner and then pops open the lid on the bottle and takes a long drink.

"Says the chef who works the fryers at a burger place."

"I may make that crap, but I don't eat it." Ben drains his shake and rinses the bottle under the tap.

"And don't get me started on your smoking," I say.

Ben rolls his eyes. "It's a stress thing, Brooks. I smoke for the same reason you run."

"Running isn't bad for you."

"It is if you get hit by a car."

"That totally wasn't my fault. And it was a nudge. I didn't even get a bruise."

He laughs and leans back against the bench. He spies the envelope. "Read it yet?" he asks.

I shake my head.

"You saw who it's from, right?"

I nod.

"And you don't want to know either way?"

I shrug.

Ben walks over and stands beside me. "It's not going to bite you, Brooks."

"You don't know that."

Ben nudges my shoulder with his. "Do you want me to look?"

I let out a breath. "I don't know."

Ben raises his eyebrow. "Someone's got to look."

"Someone already has," I reply, flipping the envelope over.

"That would explain the answering machine messages then."

"Yep." I walk around to the other side of the bench and rinse my bowl in the sink. I don't want to think about that envelope anymore. "What time do you start tomorrow?" I ask.

Ben lets me get away with the change of subject. "Not until eleven. Stavros gave Matt and I the morning off so we can work late for the community meeting tomorrow night."

"I don't know why they're bothering with it. Aren't they starting work on the site next week?"

"Yeah, but I guess they just want to let people know what's going on. There'll be a lot of construction going on for the next few weeks."

"If the tourists weren't staying away before, they'll be staying away now."

"Now, now," Ben says. "You fought it, and you lost. Be a good loser instead of a bad sport."

Ben's right, of course, but it still annoys me that he never really picked a side when we were protesting. He said he could see both sides of the argument for Scott Fisher's stupid camping development on the island and didn't really have an opinion either way. Probably because he wasn't born here. He doesn't have 'skin in the game' as my father would put it.

"Hey. Are you coming to the bonfire tomorrow night?" Ben asks, in an obvious attempt to change the subject.

I shrug. "I have to see if Rosie needs me to help out with the turtles."

"Yeah but that's not til late, right? You can come to the bonfire and then go across to help Rosie out."

"I'll see how I feel."

Ben leans in. "Jo asked if you were going." He winks at me.

I pull a face. "Ew, don't do that. It's gross."

Ben laughs. "Seriously though, Brooks. Jo's been talking about you non-stop. She's a nice girl. Though I have no idea what she sees in you, and I have no idea why you broke up with her."

"That ship has sailed," I reply. "Anyway, at least I'm not like you, getting all mushy over Nicki when she comes in to the shop and not doing anything about it. Why don't you just ask her out?"

"Because," Ben says, turning away from me and rewashing his shaker bottle. If he's trying to hide his reddening face, he's failing miserably. "She's so out of my league it's not even funny." He turns back to me.

"Besides, she's heading back to uni after summer, so what's the point?"

"You know what your dad would say?"

Ben rolls his eyes and puts on a mock-Uncle Pete voice, low and deep but a little more whiny than Uncle Pete would sound like and says, "Don't die wondering, son. Life's for living, not lazing."

"Since when does Uncle Pete have an American accent?"

Ben pokes out his tongue I laugh. "I need to get going. Some of us need to work on our figures," I say and shove Ben as I walk past.

"I'll see you in the morning," Ben calls as I head out the front door.

I'm lacing up my joggers when my parents' car pulls into the driveway. I'm relieved to see it's just my dad. I don't think I can handle another argument with my mother.

Dad pulls himself out of the driver's seat using the door as a brace. "I was hoping you were home." He hobbles around the front and leans on the bonnet. He really should get his knee looked at.

"I'm heading out for a run."

"It's going to rain again."

I shrug. "I won't melt."

Dad sighs. I can feel him watching me. He says, "Can we just talk for a minute, Brooks?"

"I'm not coming home," I say.

"I'm not here for that."

There's a first. "Then why are you here?"

"It's nice to see you too," Dad says.

"Sorry." I have to keep reminding myself that Dad's not the problem.

"Haven't you gotten any of your mum's messages? She's called at least a dozen times."

"I haven't really been here much," I lie. Dad crosses his arms and I say, "I've been taking extra shifts at the Hut to help out. I've been busy."

"Well, look. Your mother wants to see you so—"

"She sent you here?"

"No, she didn't. She doesn't know I'm here. She thinks I got called into a meeting at the bowls club." When I don't say anything he says, "I'm trying to be the peacemaker, Brooks. You know I hate it when you two fight."

"She shouldn't start them then." I put my ear buds into my ears and walk away. "I have to go."

"Brooks, wait." Dad grabs my arm. "Are you going to the community meeting tomorrow night?"

"I don't know. Why?"

"Your mother and I will be there."

Of course she will. The development's as much her baby as it is Scott Fisher's. "And?"

Dad scratches his head. "Can you not make a scene?"

I rip my ear buds out of my ears. "Are you kidding me?" Mum's the one who gets hysterical, not me. It'd be easier if I avoid her completely but it seems like Dad just wants us to play happy families. I don't want to say something I regret to Dad, because he's not the bad guy, so I just shake my head and turn to leave.

"Brooks, please. Just, at least acknowledge her tomorrow night, will you? It'd be embarrassing for her if you don't even say hello to your own mother in front of everyone. You know what this town's like."

And there it is. "See, that's the problem, isn't it? It's always about her. Never about anyone else."

"Brooks—"

"No, Dad. Just..." I sigh. "Look, if you and Mum come up tomorrow night, I'm not going to ignore you. And I will try my best to not argue with her. But I'm not going to pretend everything's fine because it's not."

Dad nods. "Fair enough."

"And for the record, she was the one who told me to go. I didn't just leave, so..."

"I know." He pats me awkwardly on the shoulder, which never used to be weird because up until the trouble between Mum and I over the development, we used to be a family of huggers. As I turn to head off, Dad says, "Enjoy your run."

"You better get to the bowls club, just in case she sends someone to check up on you," I call back, and break into a jog.

Three

Riley

When I get out of bed the next morning, the sun is shining through the window above the sink, and it's starting to feel muggy already. I kick off the sheet, sit up and stretch. When I check the time and discover that it's after nine, I realise that I've probably missed seeing Dad this morning. I remember he said something in the car last night about some big job he's got on but I didn't pay too much attention. I'm not betting on getting to see him much at all while I'm here, since him being busy with his business is the reason I stopped coming to visit him in the first place.

My stomach grumbles, and I decide to head up to the house to get some breakfast. As I open the door to the guest house, I touch the top of Mum's ashes box and think about what she said before she died.

"Promise you'll try with your dad," she'd said, and I promised because you have to when someone asks you to when they're dying. Although I have no idea if I can actually keep my promise, I decide that since it's only really for a year until I finish high school, I'll try to get along with him.

The main house is quiet and as I close the glass sliding door behind me, I feel like I'm intruding. The room I've come into is massive. It's all big white tiles and white walls. There's a black lounge and wooden dining table to my left and a blue-topped pool table on my right. The kitchen is directly in front of me, a long bright white breakfast bar separating it from the rest of the room. It feels like those designer show houses Mum and I used to look at on weekends - all shiny and new and no hint that someone actually lives in them.

As I make my way across to the kitchen, hoping someone has left me a note to tell me where to find things so I don't have to feel like I'm robbing the place, Julie appears from out of a side room.

"Oh." Her hand flutters to her chest in surprise but she smiles. "I thought I heard the door, but I just assumed it was Jason." She breezes over to me, her light dressing gown flowing out around her, and wraps me in a hug. Instead of being awkward, it actually feels good, so I hug her back.

She pulls back and holds me at arm's length. "You've gotten so big!" I must cringe because she drops her hands from my shoulders, screws up her nose and says, "Sorry. You're probably going to get that a lot over the next few weeks when you run into people around here. Do you want something to eat? You must be starving."

She turns and heads back around the bench and starts rattling off my breakfast choices as she packs the dishwasher. "There's cereal in the cupboard. There's muesli if you're into healthy stuff. Jason eats all the stuff that's full of sugar, bloody boys, and your dad just normally has toast and coffee." She looks up suddenly. "Do you drink coffee?"

I nod in reply and Julie must approve of this (unlike Mum, just saying) because she smiles broadly. "Great. I thought we could have a girls' day today since your father will be busy getting ready for the community meeting tonight and with everything else he has on his plate this week, I doubt we'll see him much at all today, although he did say he'd try to meet us for lunch." She stops and takes a breath. "Did he tell you about that?"

I'm unsure whether she's talking about lunch or the community meeting, but he never mentioned either of them so I shake my head in reply. I'd forgotten how much and how fast Julie talks. I always thought it would annoy me, but today, when I don't feel like talking anyway, I'm kind of glad she won't let me get a word in.

"Men," Julie says, swatting her hand in the air at nothing in particular. "Never tell you the important stuff. Anyway, we can talk about that over coffee at the cafe when we do some shopping after breakfast." She stops and smiles at me and I can't help but smile back.

"Breakfast," she says, like the idea has just occurred to her. "What did you say you wanted?"

"Toast is fine," I reply.

"Great," Julie says. "Bread is in the pantry," (she points to the room where she emerged from before), "as are the Vegemite, honey and peanut butter. Butter and jams are in the fridge. We've got orange juice and breakfast juice as well."

She pulls out a drawer on her side of the breakfast bar. "Cutlery is here." She opens a cupboard under the bench. "Plates and cups in here. Just trawl through the cupboards until you find what you need."

"Thanks," I finally manage to say.

"Oh, and toaster and kettle are in the stowaway cupboard beside the stove." She lifts the little roller door on the opposite bench and then turns back to me and smiles. "Once you have some breakfast, I'll give you a tour of the house, so you know your way around and then we can both get ready to go out. Okay?"

I nod. "Okay."

"Good," Julie smiles. "I'll leave you to it and go have a shower." As she walks off toward the hallway she calls back, "Make yourself at home."

"Thanks," I call back. I wait until she's out of sight and then I duck around to the other side of the bench and head to the pantry. It's the size of my study at my old house and I feel a little overwhelmed at the amount of food in there. I reach for a loaf of bread but my eye is drawn to the box of Fruitloops sitting beside the Coco Pops and Weetbix. Fruitloops were my favourite when I was a kid, and I haven't had them for ages. Not since

Mum got cancer and made us both stop eating so much processed food. I used to feel bad for lying to her about the fast food I'd get on my way home from school but I think I would've died if all I'd eaten over the last two years was lentil soup and chickpea burgers with home-made hummus. I put the bread back, grab the box of cereal and head back to the bench to find a bowl.

The sugar hit on my first bite is amazing. It reminds me of when Brooks and I used to have big bowls of cereal for dinner when we were little. Only Brooks would add a big spoonful of Quik to hers for extra flavour. No wonder we used to have so much energy when we were kids. I close my eyes and savour the taste of fake flavouring. It's so bad it's good and I almost groan out loud.

I'm so glad I don't though because as I take my next big spoonful, the sliding door opens and in walks Jason. I mean, I'm assuming it's Jason. I haven't seen him since the last time I was here because he didn't come to the funeral, and back then he was just a scrawny kid with too-long brown hair. He hasn't changed too much from the way I remember him. He's taller but he's filled out more, and his hair's still long, scruffier though and hanging down in wet ringlets around his shoulders. He's wearing a black wet suit, the top of it pulled down and hanging off his waist. He wears the surfer look pretty well. I can't believe he's almost the same age as me. "Hey," he says, like it's not strange me sitting in his kitchen. "Mum here?"

"Shower," I say around a mouthful of cereal.

He nods in reply. "Can you tell her I'm heading into town with Damo, and I'll be back after lunch?"

I nod.

"Thanks. Catchya," he says and slips back out the door. As I watch him disappear around the corner of the house, it occurs to me how everyone is acting so normal about me being here, almost like I've always been here. I'm not entirely sure why that bothers me, but it does.

When Julie said she was taking me to the new shopping centre, I imagined it being a lot bigger than it actually is. A cafe, a surf shop, a chemist, a small grocery shop and an Indian takeaway would not be classified as a shopping centre where I come from. Julie and I skirt around the cafe seating on the footpath, avoiding a waitress who's trying to clear a table, and spot the surf shop on the corner.

Julie stops to check out the messy specials table out the front. It's mostly singlets and board shorts, so I wander further inside to scout out the togs, which are closer to the back of the shop. As I head past a rack of flouro coloured clothes, I hear a familiar laugh that I wasn't expecting. I scoot around the back of the rack and peer around it to see where the laugh came from. There, serving at the counter, is Brooks Doherty.

I duck back behind the clothes rack and try to decide what to do next. She would have finished school this year because she's a year older than I am, and I thought for sure she'd be long gone by now. My mouth has gone dry at the thought of talking to her. I mean, she probably doesn't even know who I am now anyway. It's been five years and a lot has changed.

I look back over the rack and watch as Brooks rings up a sale. She's taller than I remember, obviously, but she's still sporty and broad-shouldered. I wonder if she still has her home-made weights? And oh my God, she got her eyebrow pierced, just like she said she would. I wonder what her mum said when she came home with it? She tucks a stray hair underneath her cap and laughs at something the girl says. Wait a minute, is she flirting with her?

Oh my God. Get it together, Riley. It's just Brooks. I take a deep breath and stand up.

"Riley?" Julie appears from behind me. "Everything okay?"

"Oh, sure. Yeah, I was just…" I turn back to the rack I'm standing beside and pretend I'm interested in the clothes. "I was just checking these out."

"The boys' shorts?"

"Yeah. For Jason." Good recovery.

Julie smiles, takes a pair of shorts off the rack and says, "These would look good on him, don't you think?" She holds them up and turns them around. "And he does need some new ones. I don't know what he does in his clothes, but nothing of his ever lasts long at all."

"Hi," comes a voice from beside me. I turn to see a guy dressed in fluoro yellow board shorts and a singlet, a straw fedora on his head. "Can I help you?"

"Oh. Yeah. I actually need some new togs."

"No problem," he says. "They're right over here." I leave Julie at the rack and as I follow the sales guy, I risk a look back toward the counter, but Brooks is gone.

"What are you looking for?" the guy asks.

"Huh?"

"Togs," he says. "What sort of togs are you looking for?"

"Oh, I'm not sure." I follow him over to the wall of togs and listen as he explains the virtues of each brand, and I'm glad for the distraction from my thoughts about Brooks.

Four

Brooks

I can't believe that Roly Fisher is standing in my surf shop. Well, not mine exactly, but the one I work at. For years all I could think about was Roly and that day in the storm when she was huddled against me, scared out of her mind. I mean, yeah we were only kids, and I had no idea about the feelings I was having back then, but I can remember how good it felt to have her around. Summers were so much more fun when she was in town.

Every year, a week or so after Christmas, Roly would arrive in town to see her dad. I used to go wait on the corner of the esplanade on my bike and when I'd see Scott Fisher's panel van cruise around the corner,

I'd race them back to the house, me riding on the bike path, weaving in and out of tourists and Riley hanging out the window of the car, egging me on. Sometimes Roly's mum would come up with her and they'd stay at Uncle Pete's caravan park.

As soon as they were unpacked, Roly and I would head straight down to the Burger Hut, get chocolate milkshakes and a serve of hot chips with chicken salt and sit on the beach and catch up.

Over the next couple of weeks, Roly would help me clean the cabins and the camp grounds at the caravan park, and I'd take her swimming and fishing and pumping for yabbies. We'd spend most nights playing cards in the rumpus room at the back of Uncle Pete's house and sometimes we'd help clear the tables at the Burger Hut for Gloria when she was run off her feet. Afterwards, we'd lie on our backs on the picnic table out the back of the Hut and look at the stars and stuff ourselves full of whatever was left in the hotbox.

And then one year, it all changed. The summer after the last big storm, Roly didn't turn up. When I asked Mum if she'd heard anything, she said something vague about Riley's parents fighting, which as far as I was concerned, wasn't a reason for Roly to not come back. So I snuck into the caravan park office when Uncle Pete was busy to get Roly's address from an old booking ledger and wrote to her, asking what had happened. She didn't write back.

I wrote to her every month for two years with no response. I got to the stage where I wondered if I'd made her up; if she was just a figment of my overactive twelve-year-old imagination. And now here she is, standing at a rack in the back of the shop looking at board shorts.

I mean, Dad told me about her mum dying. Heck, the whole of Roper's Beach knows about it. And it totally makes sense that she'd come back to live with her dad. I just wasn't prepared to see her so soon.

I don't think she's seen me yet so I take the chance to watch her some more. I know that sounds stalkerish but I haven't seen her in so long, I just want to make sure it's her and not some mirage I'm seeing from the heat. She's hardly changed at all, apart from not being so squishy with puppy fat. Now she looks long and lean, her denim shorts just reaching the bottom of her butt. Not that I'm checking her out or anything. I guess I should stop calling her Roly though. Her hair's still the same strawberry blonde it was back then, but instead of the pigtails she wore all the time, she's got it pulled back in a messy sort of pony tail that's just long enough to tickle her neck.

She pulls a couple of hangers off a rack, holds them up in front of her and then puts them back. I'm trying to decide whether to just walk over to her and see if she wants a hand with anything, which I should probably do because it is my job, but I wouldn't know the first thing to say to her. I mean, what do you say to someone who's mum died? Besides, I don't even know whether she remembers who I am. Before I can make up my mind, Reece jabs me in the ribs.

"Stop ogling the customers," he says, clearly ogling Roly himself.

"I'm not," I reply, but I know he knows I'm lying.

Reece leans in closer. "The chicks are the only reason I work here you know?"

As if I didn't. Reece has this stupid thing about scoring the girls who come in to the shop. If they're under a five, he won't serve them. What he fails to realise though is that anyone over a three is way out of his league.

"If you don't want her, I'll take her," he says. "She's got to be at least a seven."

I want to hit him for devaluing Roly like that but I bite my tongue.

"You can go sort out the specials table," he says when I don't answer him. I'd usually argue with him, on account of me being fifty bucks behind him on sales this month, but I just don't think I'm ready to talk to Roly just yet.

"Whatever," I shrug, and head out to the front of the shop to refold the clothes on the table that the Kennedy's messed up earlier.

Five

Riley

"I'm sorry Scott was too busy to have lunch with us." Julie stabs at her salad with a fork a few times before she finally gets a couple of leaves and a tomato on it. She crunches into it, and when she's finished she says, "He's been so busy getting everything right for the final reveal for tonight."

"What's he revealing?" I ask. I lift the top of my burger, pick off the lettuce and drop it on my plate. There's no nutritional value in it so I really have no idea why they still insist on putting it on anything, let alone a burger.

"The final plans for his camping development on the island."

I drop the bun back onto my burger and look up. "He's developing the island?"

"He hasn't told you?"

I shake my head. The island had always been this wild, untamed place that Brooks and I would paddle across to on kayaks and explore. From what I remember, it was owned by some old family who don't live in the area anymore and the only thing on it was an old tin shed that a bird watching group from Townsville used to use.

Julie puts down her fork. "Oh," she says. "Your dad's building an upmarket camping ground over there. Trying to bring in a higher level of tourists."

"Don't people camp at the caravan park?"

Julie shrugs. "Not much anymore. It's a bit run down since Pete left." She sips on her water.

"So, why is Dad building a camp ground on the island then? If no-one's camping here much anymore, I mean."

Julie puts down her fork, takes a deep breath and says, "Well", and as soon as she says 'well' I know I'm in for a long-winded explanation. I'm not disappointed. "I don't know if you know this, but Roper's has been getting fewer and fewer tourists every year. The council has always had this thing about wanting to keep it as pristine as possible, right?" She pauses and I feel like she thinks I know what she's talking about so I nod as I take a bite of my burger.

Apparently satisfied with my response, Julie continues. "Which meant that your father couldn't build anything over two stories high and no units on the beach front and a whole heap of other rules." She shakes her head. "So anyway, they did that big upgrade of the highway a few years ago, which diverted a lot of the traffic away from here, so people just don't come here on the way through to Townsville anymore.

The council let some other developer build this new shopping centre here last year to try to get more people to come. I can't repeat what your father said about that. He's been trying to do something like that for years. Anyway, the council thought providing more shopping facilities would attract more people but it didn't really work. I mean, you don't come to Roper's for shopping, do you?" Julie laughs and waves her hand like she's swatting away that thought. "So your dad had this great idea about promoting eco-tourism."

"Eco-tourism?" I ask. "Like, getting back to nature type stuff?"

"You've heard of it?" Julie asks.

"Yeah. Mum was into it."

"Right," Julie says. "So anyway, the council loved the idea, and the first thing they did was turn the old Mackenzie farm into a conservation park and..." I start to switch off as she's telling me about revegetation and the bush walks and the nature trails and then starts on the council politics of it all. By the time Julie gets back around to Dad's idea, I've finished my burger and I'm swishing my straw around in the bubbles at the bottom of my milkshake.

"So, Scott got this great idea to cater for more expensive tastes, rather than budget campers and the council loved it. He managed to talk the Fiorelli's into selling him the island, because you know they were never going to do anything with it and well, now he's developing it into an exclusive luxury campground." She picks up her fork and stabs at her salad, which I hope is a sign that she's finished talking.

Firstly, I can't believe my dad owns an island, and secondly, luxury and campground are two words that don't usually go together. Although I don't fully understand how it'll work, I don't want to risk another long-winded explanation from Julie. Instead I ask, "How's he going to get people to come here?"

"He has his ways," Julie says, mysteriously. She leans in and whispers, "He has connections in the industry who know a few famous people, so he's going to see if he can get someone on board to help sell the place. He's got a huge tourism campaign in the works." She nods. "Just wait and see. No matter what anyone says, your dad will be the one who saves Roper's."

Dad saving anyone from anything would be a first, considering he couldn't even save his first marriage.

Six

Brooks

Saturdays at The Burger Hut aren't as busy as they used to be because of the drop in tourists, but today's a lot busier than usual thanks to the extra people in town for the community meeting tonight. Apparently, half the district wants to see the final plans for Scott Fisher's camping development and they've come out to Roper's early. The meeting doesn't start until six tonight, and there are already so many people at the Hut that they're overflowing onto the grass beside the shop where the Smith house use to be.

I clear a couple of the outside tables as I pass and head around the back and into the kitchen. Ben's at the fryer, juggling baskets, dumping cooked chips into a bowl and then refilling the basket with more. I give him a bump on my way past to catch his attention. "Hey, Brooks." He wipes his forehead with the back of his arm, lifts a basket from the fryer, gives it a shake and then drops it down into the oil again.

"Hey," I reply. "Need a hand?"

"This is the busiest we've been in ages. We're getting slammed." Ben nods at the bowl of fresh chips. "Can you take those out and toss them in the hot box for me and see what needs a top up?"

"Sure." I shake some salt over the hot chips, toss them around in the bowl and take them out to the front counter. Gloria nods at me when she sees me. She's got a full house, so I dump the chips in the hot box and check the bain trays.

When I get back out to the kitchen, I tell Ben he needs to do more potato scallops and fish bites and hand him back the empty chip bowl. I take two clean trays from the stack on the bench and put them beside the fryers.

"Thanks," Ben says. "Can you get me the potato scallops from the cold room? Man, I hope Stavros hurries up."

"Where is he?" I ask as I disappear into the cold room and retrieve the bag of potato scallops.

Ben empties the bag of scallops onto a tray, tosses some into an empty basket and dumps it into the deep fryer. He turns his head away from the steam. "He had to go get something from the hardware store for the pizza ovens. He shouldn't be too far away, I hope. It's just me and Matt at the moment and," he lowers his voice, "Matt's freaking out with the burgers. It's his first time on his own."

"I can work the fryers if you want to help him with the burgers," I say.

"Nah. Matt needs the practice. He'll be right. And Jo's in soon to help Gloria and Sophie out, so we'll be good."

I look over to where Matt's flipping patties and checking on steaks and eggs. He seems to be in a pretty good rhythm so I decide against saying hi. I head back into the cold room to get the fish bites and as I come back out, Stavros rushes into the kitchen. He grabs his apron from the hook and pulls his cap down on his head. "Sorry," he says, tying his apron around his waist. "Got stuck with Mac talking about the cricket. God that man can talk." He chuckles to himself as he steps in beside Ben. "Hey, Brooks. You helping out tonight?"

"If you need me, sure."

"We'll need all hands on deck," Stavros says. "Ben and Matt are going to do all the prep, but I'll need you to help Gloria take the orders once we kick off."

"No problem. If I'm working, it means I don't have to talk to my mother."

Stavros narrows his eyes but doesn't get up me for dissing Mum. He knows the story. The whole town does. Instead he says, "Can you get here early and help Gloria set up?"

"Sure. I'll come back around five."

Stavros smiles. "Great." He pats Ben on the back, points to the fryers and says, "Get that lot out and go have your break. Don't be too long though." He pulls order tickets out of the machine, puts them onto the docket rail and heads over to the grill. "Looks like there's not going to be a let up any time soon."

I follow Ben outside and around to the back of the shop. We sit down on the bench in the shade. It's only just gone three and the air is hot and sticky. The breeze should start picking up soon to cool it down. Ben tosses me a bottle of water and stretches out beside me. "How was work?" he asks, taking out a cigarette and lighting it. He takes a long drag, blows out the smoke and leans back against the wall.

"Same as always," I reply. "Reece is still kicking my arse in sales."

"Is that why you worked late?"

"Brit was late in and Reece took off early."

"Does he even work there anymore?" Ben asks, sucking in another lung full of smoke and blowing it out high into the air.

"Being best mates with the boss has it's perks I guess."

Ben nods. "Your mum called again this morning," he says. He runs his hands through his hair and the way he looks at me, I know what's coming next. "You really need to talk to her, Brooks."

"No," I say. "I don't."

"I can't keep covering for you."

"I know."

Ben shoves me with his shoulder. "Maybe she's waving the white flag."

"I doubt it. And unless she gets off my back, I don't want to talk to her." I take a long drink of water. "Have you heard from Uncle Pete?"

"He's in Alice Springs at the moment. Bloody hot out there." Ben finishes off his cigarette and stubs it out in the pot near his feet.

Gloria sticks her head around the corner. "Stavros told me you were out here."

Ben stands up and stretches. "I better get back in there. I'll catch you back here later." He taps the top of my cap and goes back inside.

"Everything okay?" I ask. "I can stay and help if you like."

Gloria fobs me off with a wave of her hand. "Jo's just got here. We'll be fine once the early crowd leaves." She sits down beside me and smiles. "You'll never guess who I saw today."

"Probably not," I reply.

"Riley Fisher," Gloria says, like it's the name of someone famous.

I pretend I don't know who she's talking about and she shakes her head at me and says, "Don't tell me you don't remember little Riley Fisher. God, you two used to be joined at the hip."

"I remember Riley," I reply. And she's not so little anymore, I think.

"Well," Gloria says, "I heard she wasn't meant to be up here until just before Christmas but Scott flew her up early."

The whole town knew Riley was coming. The news of Riley's mum's death went through Roper's like wildfire, and of course every man and his dog were speculating what would happen with Riley.

"You should go up and see if she wants to catch up," Gloria says, not waiting for me to reply.

"I might do that if I get time," I say. "Although under the current circumstances, her dad might not let me in the yard."

Gloria shakes her head. "Who cares what Scott thinks? Riley'd probably like to see you, especially after everything that happened with her mum."

Before Gloria can plan the rest of my summer around Riley Fisher, Stavros sticks his head around the door. "Jo needs you out front, Glo."

Gloria pats my leg. "I'll see you later."

"Yeah," I reply. "I should get home anyway. I'll see you tonight."

Gloria waves me off and I throw my backpack over my shoulder and head home.

Seven

Riley

It's taken just under an hour for me to be totally over Dad's community meeting thing, and he hasn't even revealed the development plans yet. The number of people who have come up to me since we arrived to tell me how sorry they are that Mum died equals roughly half of the crowd crammed inside the Hut. I was so sick of it that by the time Mrs Harper comes over, I seriously lose it. "I'm sorry to hear about your mother," she says.

I give the required thanks and stiff smile but she doesn't go away. "Such a terrible way to go, isn't it?" she says.

I mean, what the hell am I supposed to say to that? Any way to die, as far as I can tell, is a bad way to die. I reply, "It was so sudden, you know?"

"Sudden?" Mrs Harper asks. "I thought she was sick for a while?"

"Oh, she was. And then she got better and then one day, after she was better she went to cross the road and then BOOM! She gets hit by a car."

Mrs Harper clutches at her chest with her hand. Her mouth contorts and she gapes at me wide-eyed. I almost burst out laughing at her but I know how much worse that would make things. "Oh," she says. And "Oh" again. "I, well, Mavis told me it was cancer. I'm so sorry dear. I had no idea."

Before I can say anything more, Mrs Harper hurries away, back to her friends sitting in a corner sipping on lemonade. Jason appears beside me. "What did Mrs Harper want?"

"The usual sorry to hear about your mum stuff," I reply.

Jason nods. I like that he doesn't give me any sympathy. I'm not the Girl Who's Mother Died of Cancer to him. I'm just the step-sister he hasn't seen in five years.

"Where have you been?" I ask him.

He takes a drink from a soft drink can and smiles at me. "Out the back with some mates." Why do I get the feeling something's not right?

"Are you up to something?" I ask.

He half laughs. "Nope."

"I don't believe you," I reply.

"Shh," he says. "It's about to start."

We both look over to the corner where Dad and Mrs Doherty are standing behind a box with a white sheet over it. I know it's a 3D model of the development, because Jason and I helped Dad move some of the chairs and tables out of the way this afternoon so we could fit it inside the Hut. It's actually quite impressive and I know Dad's proud of it. Julie's standing to the side. She spots us and gives us a wave.

"Welcome everyone," Dad says. "Thanks for coming. Now, I know we've been through a lot with this development and I've tried to take everyone's concerns on board throughout the whole process. Work is ready to commence on site this week, and to celebrate that I wanted to share with you a 3D model of what you can expect to see. We've tried to incorporate low-impact and eco-friendly materials with sophisticated design. Right from the start of construction, to the end product, we'll be trying to have minimum impact on the environment." He pauses and looks out over the faces in the crowd. He's searching for someone. He smiles. "And Bert, rest assured, you can still go on over to the island and bird watch, just as long as you leave your home brew at home and don't give it to any of my workers."

Bert and a few others laugh at that. Dad then turns to Brooks' mum. "I'll hand over to the Deputy Mayor, Mrs Lorraine Doherty, to say a few words."

Mrs Doherty steps forward. "Thanks, Scott. I can smell the pizzas starting to cook, so I won't say too much, except to thank Scott for helping Roper's look to the future with tourism. We all know how quiet it's been the last few years since the highway upgrade, and we can definitely use a shot in the arm. I think this new glamping development over on the island is a great step forward. It'll provide something different to tourists looking for an environmental experience, and will provide some much-needed jobs for locals too. So, without further ado." She smiles at Dad. They both take a corner of the white sheet and pull it off to the side to reveal the model.

There's some applause and then, from outside, comes yelling. I follow Dad's gaze to the outdoor eating area, where a couple of people holding signs are trying to push their way in but are being stopped by a couple of men holding them back in the doorway. I can't hear what they're saying because the glass walls are blocking most of the noise, and they're all yelling over each other.

"What's that all about?" I ask Jason.

"Some people just don't like progress," he replies. Dad looks a little uncomfortable but he ignores the people trying to get his attention and says, "The plans are here, have a look at them and I'll be happy to answer any questions you have. In the mean time, Stavros and Gloria have the pizza ovens primed and ready, so go enjoy some fresh, local-made pizza." He leans in to hear what Mrs Doherty says to him and shakes his head. They both look across the room to where Brooks is standing with Gloria, taking orders. I wonder what that's about?

Dad pushes his way through the throng of people, pulling Julie along behind him, shrugging off questions, and when they gets to us he says, "There's always someone who tries to ruin a moment."

Julie gives him a hug and kisses him on the cheek. "It's too late now. I don't know why they're still bothered with it."

"Who were they?" I ask.

Dad runs his hand through his hair. "Just some mob calling themselves Citizens of Roper's Against Glamping. They don't even know what glamping is."

"What are they protesting about?" I ask.

"Just some misunderstandings about the development. That's all. I was hoping to sort all that out tonight but some people just don't want to listen no matter what." Again, he looks over to where Gloria and Brooks are taking pizza orders. Then he looks back at me and half smiles. "I'm sorry I missed lunch today, Riles. After this thing's over, we'll spend some time together at home, yeah?"

"Okay," I reply.

"You should go and grab a pizza before it gets too busy," he says.

As I head off to stand in line, Dad is approached by a few people and gets pulled back away to the model. I watch him getting animated as he points things out on the map and talks with his hands, making wild gestures in the air, and the people around him nodding and smiling. It's pretty clear that this project means a lot to him and the people of Roper's.

Eight

Brooks

During the speeches, Jo had pointed out a few times when I was huffing, which was pretty much every time Mum or Scott Fisher said something I obviously thought was BS. She'd dug me in the ribs and told me to be quiet and once, she told me to just get over it. I hadn't even realised that I was scowling until she threatened to 'kiss it right off', which would've made me laugh a few months ago, but not now.

I know the fight about the development is over, and that it's going ahead no matter what, but it still annoys me that they're all taking Scott's word that the construction isn't going to impact on the turtles that are nesting on the island.

By seven o'clock, we're so busy with pizza orders, I don't have time to think about it anymore. There are people everywhere. Matt and Ben are tag-teaming on the pizza ovens and the prep tables and Jo and Sam are run off their feet getting the pizzas out. Gloria and I have two lines going for orders; only giving people a choice of meatlovers, ham and pineapple, plain cheese or vego has made ordering easier. Of course, not everyone is happy with the choices. Mrs McNamara made a bit of a fuss because she didn't like any of the standard toppings and in the end, Jo took her over to Matt, who was making the pizzas up, so she could create her own.

Mum waves to me over people's heads as if nothing is wrong and behind her, Dad makes a face that I guess is supposed to mean 'please don't be mean to your mother'. I get the hint, and by the time they make it to the front of the line, I'm too tired to fight.

Mum says, "It's good to see you, Brooks."

"A meatlovers and a ham and pineapple?" I reply.

"Yes, actually. Is Pete's place okay?"

"It's fine, Mum. Do you want any drinks?"

"You're getting along with Ben okay?" she asks, completely ignoring my attempt to move her on.

"We're fine."

"I'm so glad he's there. Ben was always the more mature of your cousins. Of course, it helps he's one of the oldest."

"Mum!"

"What?"

"Drinks?"

"Oh. Just a bottle of water," Mum says. "And can you make sure there's no onion on that meatlovers? Your dad's been getting indigestion."

I resist the urge to roll my eyes. "There's no onion on the meatlovers, Mum."

"Okay, good."

"Anything else?"

"No, thank you."

I finish writing up the order docket, rip off the number at the bottom and hand it to Mum. "Shouldn't be too long."

She takes the number and as I look behind her to the next person in line, she says, "Brooks, we need to talk."

"Not now, Mum. I'm busy."

She looks at me and purses her lips. She leans toward me and just loud enough for me to hear asks, "Just, I have to ask. That fracas earlier, you didn't have anything to—"

I cut her off. "You think I organised a protest? Jesus, Mum." I shake my head. "I need to take more orders. Can you go wait for your pizza?"

She looks like she doesn't believe me, but rather than argue, she lifts her head higher and says, loud enough for the people around her to hear, "Thank you, darling. I'll see you later."

I ignore her and take the next order. When I look up again, I see that Riley's standing in my line, a couple of people back from the front. It throws me a little. I mean, I thought she might be here because this is her dad's thing, but I'm still not sure what I'm going to say to her. I mean, I have no idea whether Scott's told her about C.R.A.G or not, and if he has, what she even thinks about it. I guess I'm about to find out. I serve the next couple of people and then Riley steps up. She's smiling, which I guess is a good sign.

"Hey, Brooks," she says.

"Hey, Riley. Good to see you." All of a sudden, my palms have gone sweaty. I wipe them on my shorts.

"You too," Riley says. "Busy night?"

"Yeah. What can I get you?"

Riley's face goes blank. "Oh. I hadn't really decided."

"You got in line without deciding what you want?"

"I thought I'd know by the time I got up here." She pulls a face. "Sorry."

I can see people shifting in the line behind Riley and as much as I want to stand here and keep talking to her I say, "That's okay. How about I surprise you?"

"Really?"

"Yeah how hard can it be? There's only really three choices, right? Unless you've turned vegetarian in the last few years."

Riley laughs. "No. I haven't. Not that my mother didn't try."

"Really?" I couldn't imagine Riley, lover of hamburgers (or she was when I used to know her) not being able to eat meat.

"Yeah," Riley says. "Don't ask."

"Right, so that rules one of the choices out at least. And if I remember correctly, you don't like pineapple."

Riley nods. "Still true."

"We're down to two choices then." I write up the ticket. "One surprise pizza coming up."

"How much?" Riley asks.

"Nothing."

"You're giving me a freebie?" Riley asks, eyebrows raised.

I laugh. "No. Your dad's paid for all of this. Everyone's pizza is free tonight."

"Oh." She looks disappointed.

"I would give you a freebie anyway, if you had to pay," I say quickly.

Riley gives me a half smile. She tucks the money she was holding into her pocket. "I might catch you later then."

"Yeah," I reply. I watch as she wanders off and realise too late that she's not taken her number. "Hey, Riley," I call. She turns and I hold up the number. "You need this to get your pizza."

She laughs and pushes her way back through the crowd. "Thanks. Sorry."

"No problems. I hope you like it."

"I'm sure I will." She smiles and heads off.

Not long after, when the crowd has finally thinned out, Jo appears beside me, presents me with a bottle of Fanta and a pizza box and says, "Ben's made you a cheese pizza. Go and take a break. I'll help Gloria out."

"Thanks." I take the drink and pizza, silently cursing the she knows me so well to get me what she did, and head out to the picnic table around the back. Just talking to Riley after so long has given me a bit of a

buzz. I hope she sticks around a bit longer so I can talk
to her some more.

Nine

Riley

"Hey, it's Riley. Right?"

I turn to see who's talking to me. It's the guy who served me at the surf shop this morning. "Yeah. Hi," I reply.

"Hi. I'm Reece," he says, smiling at me. "I served you today at the surf shop."

I smile back politely. "I remember."

"Waiting for your pizza?" Reece asks.

"Yep." When you live in a city, you tend to forget how overly friendly small town people can be. Reece is obviously no exception.

"What did you get?" he asks.

"I don't know," I reply.

"You don't know?"

"Brooks ordered it for me." I'm hoping my short answers will make him go away.

"Brooks did? Do you know Brooks?"

He seems surprised.

"We used to hang out when we were kids."

"Oh. She never mentioned that. So you've been to Roper's before?"

"I used to come up here when I was a kid. My dad lives here."

"Oh? Who's your dad?"

"Scott Fisher," I reply. He's obviously not a local if he doesn't know I'm related to the infamous Scott Fisher.

Reece shifts on his feet. "Scott Fisher's your dad?"

"Yeah. Why?" It's the second time tonight I've had the feeling someone doesn't like him.

"Oh. Nothing," Reece says. "So, how long have you known Brooks then?"

I shrug. "Since we were five maybe."

"Oh, really? That long?"

I just nod. I look over to the counter where Brooks was taking orders, but she's gone.

"You're practically a local then, huh?" He smiles at me, but I don't smile back. "So you'll know about the Saturday night bonfires then."

"I guess."

"Well, there's one on tonight, if you're interested."

I turn to face him. "I doubt my father would let me go. He's pretty protective, you know?"

"Right," Reece says. He looks back over the crowd of people inside the cafe, obviously checking where Dad is.

Thankfully my number is called out before he can ask any more questions. "That's me," I say. "Catch you later."

After I get my pizza, I scan the crowd and spot Dad and Julie talking to a couple of official looking men in suits, who look out of place amongst the locals, who are mostly wearing short-sleeved shirts and shorts. Jason's sitting at a table nearby with some boys who look like they're around his age, all of them hunched over a handheld game. I decide to get some fresh air, so I head outside to see if there are any tables free to eat by myself. They all look full, and I wonder whether the old picnic table is still around the back of the Hut. No-one except the staff would know about it, so I head through the marquee down the side of the shop.

When I round the corner, I spot Brooks sitting by herself. I stand for a minute, not sure if I should go over, and then Brooks spots me.

"Riley?"

"Hey, Brooks."

"Hey," she says. "Did you see what I got you?"

I look down at my pizza box. "No. Not yet." Brooks pats the seat beside her and I go over and sit down. I open the box and peer inside. "A ham and cheese?"

Brooks grins. "Yep. You don't like all that meat on the meatlovers right? So I got you ham without the pineapple. And extra cheese." She grins.

"I thought you could only order what was on the menu tonight?"

"I put my initials on the bottom so the boys would know the order was from me so they'd make up exactly what I said."

I smile and pick up a slice. "Thanks."

"No problems."

We both eat our pizzas in silence for a bit, and I can't help looking over at Brooks every now and then. It feels familiar to be sitting beside her again, but also strange.

"How'd you end up out here?" Brooks asks eventually.

"It got a bit too loud in there, and I needed some fresh air."

"Your dad won't miss you?"

I shrug. "Not really. He's busy schmoozing."

"Yeah," Brooks says. "These council things are always boring."

"You've been to one before?"

Brooks nods. "When your mother's the Deputy Mayor, you're kind of expected to go."

"Right," I say. "I also think that guy from your work, Reece, was trying to hit on me."

Brooks snorts. "Really?"

"Yeah. When I was waiting for my pizza. He just came up to me and started talking to me, like he knew me."

Brooks shakes her head. "Well, you can't blame him."

"What do you mean?"

"Come on, Riles. Look how you've turned out. You were cute when you were a kid, but now you're all grown up. I'm sure boys just throw themselves at you."

Brooks' face is in shadow so I can't really tell if she's joking. I think she is, so I whack her on the arm. It feels like we've slipped straight back to old times. I didn't realise how much I needed that until right now.

Brooks laughs. "It's been a long time, huh?"

I nod. "Yeah. It has. So how have you been?"

"Me? I'm good. How about you?"

I don't know if she's asking in general terms, or about Mum's death, so I opt for the reply everyone expects. "I'm okay."

"Did you find what you were looking for this morning?" she asks.

"What do you mean?"

"At the shop," Brooks says. "Sorry I didn't get to talk to you. Reece keeps us busy."

I wave her off. "Oh. Sure. No problem. And yeah, I bought some new togs and stuff."

"That's good," Brooks says.

"Yeah," I reply. "I needed new ones."

There's an awkward silence and then when Brooks turns back to her pizza, the light from the shop glints off her eye. "You got your eyebrow ring then?" I ask, looking for something, anything, to keep Brooks talking. I never realised how much I missed talking to her.

Brooks touches her finger to her eyebrow. "Yeah. Hurt like hell, too." She smiles.

"What did your mum say?"

"You don't want to know." Brooks laughs. "But that argument was nothing compared to what she did when she found out about the tattoo."

"You got a tattoo? When?"

"Last year. One of Ben's mates is a tattoo artist just starting out. He did it for me for nothing for my birthday."

Before I realise what I'm saying, I blurt out, "Can I see it?"

Brooks laughs. "I'm not sure whether I want to show you or not."

"Oh. I didn't mean… If it's not somewhere you can show me that's okay." God, how embarrassing. What if it's on her boob or her butt or something?

"It's hard to see in this light," Brooks explains.

I hope Brooks can't see my face in this light so she won't notice how red I've gone. "That's okay. You can show me some other time."

I take a bite of my pizza, mainly to stop myself from saying anything else stupid.

"So how's it going being back here?" Brooks asks.

"It's okay," I say around chewing my pizza.

"You're dad must be happy you're back up here. I mean, not under the circumstances, obviously." She scrunches up her nose and shakes her head. "Sorry."

"It's okay," I shrug. I think about Brooks' question. Is Dad happy I'm back? He hasn't said anything to me really. "I don't know what Dad thinks about me being here," I say. "I haven't seen him much since I got here."

"Really?"

"Yeah. He's got his big glamping project to keep him busy."

"Right," Brooks says.

"And he's got me staying out in the guest house, which totally sucks."

"Why does that suck? You have your own space. I would be so happy if my parents had a guest house for me to stay in. Although it doesn't really matter since I'm not living there anymore." Brooks rolls up a slice of her pizza and bites into it. She hasn't changed at all.

"You're not at home?"

Brooks finishes eating her pizza and wipes her hand across her mouth. "Nope. I'm staying with Ben at Uncle Pete's."

"Oh? Why?"

Brooks shrugs. "I just needed some space. Mum and I had some pretty major arguments over your dad's development."

This surprises me. "You don't like it?"

Brooks sighs and looks like she's trying to think of a good answer. Before she can reply, someone calls her name. She turns to see who it is. "Hey, Ben. What's up?"

"Sorry to interrupt," he says. "We've just taken final orders. Can you come give us a hand to start clearing up?"

Brooks checks her watch. "Shit. Have we been out here that long?"

"Gloria came out here earlier and saw you were busy, and she didn't want to interrupt."

"Sorry," Brooks says.

Ben shrugs. "That's okay. We had it covered."

"Thanks. Hey, have you met Riley?"

"Nope." He sticks out his hand and I shake it.

"Hi," I say, and look at Brooks for an explanation.

"Ben's my cousin. He moved up here last year."

"This is your friend from when you were a kid," Ben says. "Nice to finally meet you, Riley. Brooks has told me heaps about you."

"Has she?"

He laughs. "Not really. She keeps her life BB pretty secret."

"BB?" I ask.

"Before Ben," Ben explains.

Brooks slaps at him. "Don't be so embarrassing."

"So are you coming to help out? The sooner we can get everything finalised and then packed up the sooner we can get to the bonfire. Hey," he says turning to me. "You should totally come."

"Oh, I don't know. I'd have to ask Dad. I think he wants us to spend some time together after the meeting finishes."

"You don't have to come," Brooks says. "But it would be great to catch up. If you're up to it."

"I'll find out," I reply.

Brooks stands up. "We'll be an hour or so cleaning up and then we'll head home to get changed. We should be down there by nine. It's straight down in front of the Lion's Park, where we used to have them. Be great if you can make it."

She smiles, and even though she's changed a lot, she still has the same goofy grin she used to have permanently on her face when we were kids. I can't help but smile back "Okay, sure. I'll see how I go." I watch as she heads off with Ben. I can't hear what she's saying to him, but she shoves him and he throws back his head and laughs. Brooks looks back and waves, and I wave back. Dad did tell me I could come and go as I please I guess, and spending some time catching up with Brooks isn't the worst thing I could think of to be doing tonight.

Ten

Brooks

I have to admit, when Jason arrived at the bonfire without Riley, I was a little disappointed, but I guess she wants to spend time with her dad. Which is understandable really. She hasn't seen him in a long time. Jo sits down beside me and hands me a can of soft drink.

I take the drink from her and as I bring it up to my mouth I take a sniff, just to make sure she hasn't added any alcohol. She doesn't notice, thankfully, and it seems to be okay, so I take a drink. "Thanks."

"No problem."

She's sitting a little too close to me for comfort but if I move, she'll get the shits so I just sit there with her invading my space, hoping that my lack of interaction with her will make her go away. It doesn't.

"No turtles tonight?" she asks.

"Rosie didn't call, so she must have enough people."

"You know I could help out, if you ever need more people."

"I'll let Rosie know."

There's a silence that's probably more awkward for Jo than it is for me. I'm just glad she's not wanting to talk about our so-called relationship again. I watch as Ben entertains Nicki and Sam and a few of his other friends with whatever story he's telling. He gets so animated. Uncle Pete used to joke that he must have Italian in him the way he throws his hands around in wild gestures when he talks. Whatever it is he's talking about, Nicki is completely smitten with him. I can tell by the way she looks at him, lapping up everything he says, and the way she flicks her hair back whenever Ben looks at her. And when she's talking to him, she touches his arm. I can't believe he can be so clueless. I'm going to have to do something about that I think, before she gets tired of waiting for him to get the hint and moves on.

Jo touches my arm. "Did you see that protest tonight? Scott was livid."

I shrug. "I don't know why they bothered with it. It's not like it's going to make a difference now."

"It would've made a difference if more people had turned up," Jo says.

"What do you mean?"

"Albie put the call out on Facebook for people to come and make some noise. Just one last time, you know? He had around twenty people who were supposed to come down from Townsville for it but they didn't turn up."

I turn to face Jo. "Wait a minute. You knew about the protest?"

"Yeah. Of course. I thought we could stir Scott up a bit. We're trying to come up with something to do when the Minister comes up for the sod-turning ceremony, so if you've got any ideas, we'd be happy to hear them."

"No, I don't," I say. "And the protesting is over. I can't believe you're still doing this. It's over, and there's nothing we can do about it now."

"Of course there is. It gives us a chance to let him know we're still not happy, no matter what the council says."

I stand up and face her. "You do know my mother thought I was the one who organised that little protest tonight?"

"No, I didn't. Why does that matter?"

"Because the protest group was my idea, and you've got no right to just start organising stuff without telling me, especially since we all decided to give it up once the plans were passed."

"No, you decided," Jo shoots back. "And the rest of us decided that just because you were happy to compromise your principles, we weren't."

Before I can say anything about Jo's hypocrisy about principles, Jason interrupts us. "You better come sort Corey out," he says. "He's getting rowdy."

"Damn it," Jo says. We follow Jason over to where Jo's brother, Corey, is jumping around, calling on someone to pick a fight with him. Jo sighs. She walks up to him and grabs him by the shoulder and spins him around.

"Oh, hey," Corey says, a drunken grin plastered on his face. "None of these losers can beat me." He turns back to the boys who are supposed to be his mates. "Chickens," he taunts them. "Buck, buck, buck." And then he laughs and almost falls over his own feet.

"You've been drinking," Jo says.

"You've been drinking," Corey spits back.

"I'm old enough," Jo replies. "You, on the other hand, are not."

"Who cares?" Corey says. He tries to cross his arms in defiance, but they're like jelly and they slip through each other so they just hang at his side.

Jo turns on Corey's friends. "You're all supposed to look after each other. What the hell are you thinking?"

There are a lot of non-committal shrugs and no answers. I decide to step in before Jo loses her temper and makes things worse. "We should get him home," I suggest.

"Mum and Dad are going to kill us both," Jo says. She turns to me. "I can't take him home like this. There's no way we'll get past Mum and Dad with him sloshed."

I think on that for a minute. "We'll just have to sober him up then."

"How are we going to do that?" Jo asks.

I grab Corey by the arm and pull him toward the water. "Corey and I are going for a little swim."

"What? No way!" Corey protests, but he's so drunk that he's lost all of his bodily strength. Hopefully the chill of the water will sober him up enough so we can get him home.

"Well that was a fun night, right?" I say as we walk back up the road to Jo's place. Corey is more sober than he was before, but not completely, so we're still practically carrying him along with us as he drags his feet. He's borrowed a towel from someone at the bonfire but he's still shivering. It's a warm night but the breeze will be making Corey's clothes feel like he's wearing an air conditioner.

I have a little bit of sympathy for him, but Jo obviously doesn't. I can tell by the way she's been scowling the whole way home. She tips up the water bottle in Corey's hand and for the hundredth time says, "Drink."

He does as he's told. He's not fighting us anymore at least, and I'm willing to bet that's because he's starting to feel hungover and sick. I know how he feels.

When we get a few houses away from Jo's place, I stop.

"What's up?" Jo asks.

"We need to see if Corey can walk by himself. If he can walk by himself, getting him inside without your parents suspecting will be much easier."

Jo lets Corey go on her side and I pull my arm away from him on mine. Corey stands, his head down, his shoulders slumped. "Good start. He can stand up by himself at least. Can you walk?" I ask him.

He mumbles something incoherent.

"Come on," Jo says. "Just try a few steps."

Corey shuffles forward and I have to stifle a giggle. Jo shoots me a look. "What?" I shrug. "He looks like a zombie."

"Yeah, well, he's going to feel like one in the morning," she replies.

"So not funny," Corey says. He groans and doubles over. "I think I'm going to be sick."

Jo and I grab him under the armpits and drag him off the road and into the nearest garden. Jo walks away leaving me with Corey. "Sorry," she says. "I'm a sympathetic spewer." She gags and I almost laugh. Beside me, Corey throws up what I hope is most of the stuff he drank tonight. "Get it all out, mate. You'll feel much better in the morning."

When he's done, and as soon as Jo's composed herself and is sure she's not going to throw up too, we haul Corey to his feet.

"Better?" I ask him. He nods. "Good. Let's get you home. And if you don't want to get into trouble, you have to do exactly what we say, right?"

Corey nods again. Jo hands him the water bottle and he sips from it, gasping after every small drink.

"Will your parents be up?" I ask Jo.

"Maybe," Jo replies. "I don't know. It depends what movies are on TV tonight."

"Right. So let's plan for worst case scenario, that your folks are awake." I think for a minute, trying to remember the layout of Jo's house. The stairs to the bedrooms are at the end of the entrance hallway, which means we have to get Jason past the lounge room on the right where her parents may or may not be still awake. "So," I say, "plan of attack. You can't hold him up and help him walk. That will be a dead giveaway."

"Okay," Jo says.

"You're going to walk the rest of the way to your house by yourself, okay?" I say to Corey. "Just to make sure you can make it to bed without any help."

Corey nods.

"If your parents up are up, Jo, you'll have to distract them somehow so Corey can get past without them suspecting."

Jo nods. "Got it."

We let Corey go to see if he can walk by himself. Thankfully, he manages to not trip over his own feet, although he's not looking where he's going since he's looking at the ground, so Jo and I have to steer him around a couple of wheelie bins and guide him through the gate at their house. We all sneak down the path to the front door, and Jo says, "There aren't any lights on in the lounge room. Looks like we're lucky."

"Great," I say, relieved for them both. Jo's parents are pretty good, but Corey can be a real pain in the arse for them so they'd come down pretty hard if they found out how much he's had to drink tonight.

Jo opens the door and pushes Corey inside with instructions to go straight upstairs to his room. "I'll bring you a bucket in a minute," she whispers after him. He grunts in reply.

She turns back to me. "Thanks, Brooks. I would've just let him suffer."

I shrug. "No problem. I know he can be a pain, but he's alright."

Out of the blue, Jo pulls me into a hug. When she pulls back she kisses me. It takes me by surprise. Not that I haven't kissed her before, because I have. Lots of times in fact. It's just totally unexpected because we're supposed to be over.

I pull away and step back.

"Brooks," she says, her voice husky. "I—"

"No," I say, cutting off whatever it is she wants to say to me, because I don't want to hear it. "I can't believe you. First you take over my protest group behind my back, and now you expect me to forget everything else that happened and kiss you?"

"You still like me though, right?" She runs her hand down my arm. I don't mean to but I flinch. She pulls back and crosses her arms. "Fine," she says. "Just go."

"Are we really going to do this again?" I ask.

She puts her hand up in front of her, like a shield. "I get it. You want to play around. Well some of us want to grow up and be adults."

I have no idea what she's going on about, which is just like all the arguments Jo and I have had about our on-again-off-again relationship, which has been off for nearly three months. It's too late to argue so I turn and walk away. "I'll see you around," I say. If it wasn't so late at night, I know Jo would have slammed the door shut in my face, just to make a point, but she won't risk waking her parents for the sake of one argument with me.

Eleven

Riley

You really don't realise how much stuff you have until you're standing in front of a shipping container full of boxes. The removalists dropped it off early this morning and they want to come back this afternoon to pick it up, but I have no idea what I'm going to do with it all.

I just assumed Dad would get rid of the furniture and a lot of Mum's stuff, but according to Julie, he didn't know what I wanted to keep and what I didn't so he just organised for it all to be packed up and shipped here. I have no idea what's in any of the boxes because I didn't pack them and I have no idea where I'm going to put it all considering this isn't my house. I don't even know if I want any of it.

Jason walks over and stands beside me. He whistles. "That's a lot of stuff. It's all yours?"

"Me and Mums, yeah."

"What are you going to do with it?"

"I've got no idea." Julie can't help because she's got some craft class on in town, and Dad has some of his construction equipment and machinery being taken over to the island on a barge today, so he's busy with that.

Jason crunches on a spoonful of cereal. "Me and Damo can give you a hand to shift it," he says. "If you like."

I look at him and smile. "Thanks."

"No worries. I'll ask Mum where she wants it and then we can get started. The shed's probably best, but we'll have to move Scott's old building stuff out of the way." He eats some more cereal and steps forward, peering into the container. He turns back and heads into the house. "I'll go call Damo," he calls over his shoulder.

We stack the furniture up in the shed, and most of the boxes are going into the guest room so I can go through them and decide what, if anything, I want to keep. It sounds terrible, but after watching my mother die, and spending our last year together trying to tick things off her bucket list, you realise that stuff is just stuff. With the exception of the photo albums and the ashes box, which I'm sitting on the lounge holding right now, I don't think I want to keep much at all.

Damo carries a couple of smaller boxes in and stacks them on top of a pile behind the door. "That's the last of the boxes," he says. He wipes the sweat from his face and takes a couple of steps towards me. "Hey, cool box."

I instinctively pull the box away and hold it in my lap, covering it with my hands.

"Sorry," he says, apparently getting the hint. "I just like wood. I make stuff with it." He scratches the back of his head and looks around the room.

Thankfully, Jason appears in the doorway. "Hey. We're all done. You want to head down to the beach for a swim?"

"Count me in," Damo says. "I'll take the bike and meet you down there." He pushes past Jason out the door.

"I think I'll just hang around here," I reply, looking down at the box.

"You sure?" Jason presses. "There's normally a touch game down on the beach on Sundays. Brooks'll be down there."

When I look up he smiles at me, and without me having to ask the question he says, "Mum told me you and Brooks used to be friends when you were kids. Plus, I saw you two talking last night, so I thought you might want to catch up with her."

I think on that for a minute. It would be good to see her when she's not working. I place the ashes box on the coffee table and stand up. "Give me a few minutes to get changed?"

Jason grins. "No worries. See you out front."

It doesn't take long on our walk to the beach to get sweaty and sticky. I wipe the back of my neck with my towel.

Jason takes his sunglasses off, cleans them with the bottom of his shirt and puts them back on. "Supposed to be storms coming." He cuts across the road onto the beach side. "What's it like being back?"

I follow him over. "A bit weird," I reply.

"Is it the same?"

"Yes and no."

"How's it the same?"

"Well, the Burger Hut is still here."

"It wouldn't be Roper's without the Hut," Jason says, smiling. "What's different?"

I look over at the new houses on the esplanade that have taken the place of the beach shacks as we pass them. "The houses are different. It used to feel so quiet. Now it feels, I don't know."

"Exclusive?" Jason suggests. "Expensive?"

I nod. "Yeah, I guess."

"I think so too," Jason says.

"You don't like all the new stuff?" I ask.

Jason shrugs. "People from out of town own most of the new houses now, and they don't even live in them. They're only up here a few weeks of the year, and since people stopped coming, most of the houses stay empty most of the time."

"Is that why Dad's so busy? Did he build those houses?" I ask.

"Some of them," Jason says. "Not all of them though."

As we head up and over the dune, I ask, "Has he always been this busy? Like, getting called away and not really being home?"

"For as long as I can remember," Jason replies.

"And you're okay with that?"

Jason shrugs. "You get used to it."

"How do you and Julie get to spend any time with him?"

"I learned to paddle board," Jason says. He slings his towel over his other shoulder and leads me down onto the sand.

I'm a little confused. "What does that mean?"

Jason tosses his towel onto the sand, picks up the sunscreen and starts lathering it on. "Scott loves paddle boarding, and Mum told me if I wanted to spend time with him, I'd have to learn how to fit in with him. So I got him to teach me."

"Do you like it?"

Jason laughs. "I do now." He tucks his hair behind his ears. "I hated it at first because I just couldn't get my balance, but after I got the hang of it, I kinda got why he'd go out in the mornings before work most days." He looks up at me and smiles. "You should come out with us one morning. See how you go. Julie's got a board she hardly ever uses."

"I'll see," I reply. "It's never really been my thing."

"It wasn't my thing either," Jason says with a grin.

Someone calls out to us from down on the beach. I can't see who it is, because they're so far away, but I think I can see Brooks and Ben, and I think Reece from the surf shop is there too. I don't recognise anyone else.

"Are you going to come and play?" Jason asks.

"I don't really know how to," I reply.

"It's not too hard. It's just beach touch. We make up the rules as we go."

I watch as Ben takes a pass from someone and then gets tackled by Brooks. It's a pretty mean tackle and when he gets back up, they wrestle with each other.

"You know she made Australian School Girls for footy?"

"No, I didn't," I reply.

"Yeah. She missed out on the tour though because she got expelled." As Jason says that, Reece spots us and waves us down. "Coming?" Jason asks.

I sit down on the sand. "I'll just watch for a bit. I'll mind your stuff."

"Whatever," Jason says and runs off down the sand. As I watch him run around with the others, I get a twinge of something. Jealousy maybe? He looks so at home with everyone, even though he wasn't born here, like I was. Watching them all together, wrestling and tackling and fooling around, I get a glimpse of what life could have been like if Mum and Dad hadn't gotten divorced, and I hadn't moved away when I was three. Maybe what it could've been like if I'd kept coming to visit Dad instead of just not coming back after the last time.

Twelve

Brooks

I pick up the ball to start again and before I can even tap it, Reece comes in from the side and dumps me. Arsehole. He's showing off to the girls. Probably Riley too. I pick myself up and threaten to throw the ball at his head. He puts his hands up in protest. "Hey. I thought we were playing again."

I look over at Riley, sitting up on the dune by herself. I toss the ball to Jason. "I need a break. Back in a sec."

I jog over to where Riley is sitting, shielding her eyes to look up at me. I sit down beside her so she doesn't have to look up into the sun. "Thanks," she says, dropping her hand and pushing her sunglasses on top of her head.

"Are you coming down? Jo's heading to work soon, so we could use another player."

"Nah. I'm happy just watching."

"Are you sure? Reece would love a chance to show off to you properly." I wiggle my eyebrows and Riley shoves me and laughs. I push my sunglasses up on top of my head, and all of a sudden, Riley grabs my wrist.

"This is your tattoo?" she asks, pointing at my wrist.

"Yeah." I wonder if she'll get its meaning.

She turns my hand over in hers and inspects the tattoo that circles my wrist. "What is it? A wrist band?"

"Yeah, sort of."

"Does it have any meaning?" she asks.

The fact that she's asked that means she doesn't remember. I'm not surprised. "I just liked the design," I reply, trying not to sound disappointed that she doesn't recognise it.

"I like it," she says, smiling up at me.

I pull my hand away and change the subject. "So, Jason says your stuff arrived this morning."

Riley nods.

"Unpacked yet?"

"Not yet. It's going to take ages." She picks at a stray thread on her beach towel.

"Everything okay?"

Riley shrugs. "Yeah. I just didn't realise Dad would get everything sent up, that's all."

"What else would he have done with it?"

"I don't know. Donated it to charity maybe."

"You don't want all your stuff?" I ask. Even though I'm arguing with Mum, I reckon it would be hard to throw anything out if she died.

"I don't know," Riley replies. "I guess I just thought Dad would deal with it, you know?"

"If you want a hand to go through it all, I've got tomorrow off from work. I'd be happy to come and give you a hand."

Riley smiles. "That would actually be great. You can be like those people on Storage Hoarders and tell me what I should keep and what I should get rid of."

"You watch that show too?" I ask.

Riley grins. "I love it when the hoarders are trying to justify why they need all those old newspapers."

I nod. "I know, right? I mean, how are they even going to sit and read them anyway when all their chairs are covered in other crap."

Riley laughs. There's a squeal from down on the beach and we both look over to see Reece is carrying one of the girls (it's either Nicki or Jo, I can't tell from here) down toward the water. "Oh no. Looks like Reece has moved on already." Riley jabs me and I laugh. "You should come down. I'll give you some pointers. I know how crappy you are at sport."

"Hey," she says. "What are you trying to say?"

"Oh come on. You could beat me at board games, but you weren't even in my league when it came to outside stuff." I'm deliberately baiting her, because if I remember correctly, even though Riley wasn't very co-ordinated, she was competitive. It works.

"Challenge accepted," Riley says, leaping up off her towel. "Don't say you weren't warned."

Riley decides to play on the other team. I guess she wants to prove a point. Jason taps the ball and takes a couple of steps before passing off to me. I only take a couple of steps before Ben reaches out and grabs me around the waist and swings me around. As I try to wriggle out from his grip, I manage to get a quick pass off to Damo, who gets a couple of metres away before Reece ankle taps him and he falls flat on his face into the sand. The ball bobbles out of his hands, so it's a turnover.

Reece starts again and passes off to Riley who's in front of me. She handles it like a hot potato and throws it to no-one as soon as she gets it. It lands in the sand and she screws up her face. "Sorry. I panicked."

"So you should with me about to tackle you," I say as I pick up the ball and walk past her. She goes to give me a shove but I duck out of her way and she misses. She pokes her tongue out at me and pulls a face.

I tap the ball and pass it off to Jason. He does a big right foot step and makes Reece look like an idiot, which is never hard, and takes off. When Ben is just about to intercept him, Jason tosses the ball backwards, high into the air. It loops up and over both his and Ben's heads and I manage to scoop it up, just before it hits the ground. There's nothing but space in front of me, so I take off up the sand toward the try line. I chance a look behind me and I'm surprised to see Riley sprinting after me, grinning. She's gaining on me too, and I can't make my legs go any faster.

I can hear her heavy breathing when she gets close to me, and when she takes her first grab at me, and then we're tumbling onto the sand in a laughing, panting heap. She half lands on top of me and through her giggles she asks if I'm okay.

"I'm good," I say, panting and spitting out sand. We look at each other, grinning and when our eyes meet, the world tilts. I don't know what Riley feels at that moment, or even if she feels it, but my heart stops, just for a second. I'm hyper-aware of her hand resting on the skin of my stomach, and I feel like I'm seeing her for the first time. It's amazing and weird and confusing, all at once. We just lay there looking at each other for what feels like ages but what must only be seconds, panting and sucking in breaths.

She pulls her hand away from me and gets up. "Sorry," she mumbles. She brushes herself off and then offers me her hand. I take it and she hauls me up.

"Great tackle," I say.

"Thanks," she replies, but she can't look at me. Shit.

I try again. "You're faster than you look."

That gets me a cheeky grin. "What? I don't look fast?"

"Like I said, you were never the sporty one," I say, and she shoves me as we head back over to the others.

Ben jogs over to us. "I've got to get going," he says. "Nicki and I are going to grab a drink and go over the new pizza menu before work."

"Oh, really?" I say.

"Yeah," Ben replies. "Please don't be a dick about it."

As he turns to walk away I call out, "So, should I expect you home after work tonight?"

Ben gives me the finger and I wave him off.

"I could do with a drink myself," Riley says.

"Milkshakes?"

"Perfect," she says. "After I get rid of all this sand." She brushes at it but it's sticky stuff.

"Only one way to get that off," I say, and take her hand and pull her down to the water.

Thirteen

Riley

A man comes in to the Hut dressed in construction clothes and I notice that Brooks is scowling all of a sudden. He's got a big, booming voice, so we can hear the conversation he has with Gloria at the counter, and when he says he has to wait until high tide to get the barge over to the island, Brooks mumbles, "I hope it gets stuck." She stabs her straw into her milkshake a couple of times and then takes a long drink.

"You really don't like what Dad's doing over on the island, do you?"

"What?" Brooks looks surprised I heard her. "Oh, you know. It's no big deal."

"Obviously it is," I say. "I get the feeling a few people don't like what he's doing, but I don't understand why it's a problem. I mean from what I've seen, Roper's isn't exactly full of tourists anymore, is it?"

Brooks looks around at the empty tables. "It's only early in the season. Most people don't come up til after Christmas."

I know that's not true, and I know something is obviously bothering her about Dad's development, but I don't want to push her so I change the subject to something I know she'll like talking about - herself. "Jason told me you made the Australian team for football. I didn't know you were that into it."

Brooks looks up and her whole demeanour has changed. She's more relaxed and she gives me a broad smile. She doesn't answer my question, but instead asks, "What did Jason tell you?"

"Just that you were good enough to make some tour but didn't go." I leave the rest of what he told me hanging, just to see if she'll tell me herself.

She purses her lips. "Uh-huh."

I laugh. "Okay, okay. He told me you got expelled and that's why you missed out. Is that true?"

Brooks nods. "Yep."

"I can't believe it. You? Expelled from school?"

"Yeah," she shrugs. "It's no biggie."

"No biggie? Does that mean you haven't officially finished high school then?"

Brooks takes a deep breath and lets it out. "We're negotiating on that actually."

"What's to negotiate?"

"Whether I get to just sit exams next year to graduate or whether I have to repeat."

"Wow. It's that bad?"

Brooks nods. She drains the rest of her milkshake and leans back in her seat.

A thought occurs to me. "You know, if you have to repeat, that would mean we'd be doing final year together."

Brooks laughs. "Always the optimist," she says.

"Hey, I was thinking more about me than you. I won't know anyone there except for Jason, and if you're there, well, at least I'll know one more person."

Brooks gets all serious. "Probably better for you if pretended that you didn't know me."

"What's that supposed to mean?"

Before she can answer, Jo comes over and puts her hand on Brooks' shoulder. Brooks visibly tenses. "Hey," Jo says. "How were the milkshakes?"

"Great," I reply.

"Fine," Brooks deadpans.

"Great," Jo says. She looks over at me. "So, Riley. Are you enjoying being back at Roper's?"

"It's alright so far," I reply. I'm getting the feeling something's going on between Jo and Brooks but I'm not exactly sure what it is.

"Cool," Jo says. "I guess I should get back to it." She leans in close to Brooks. "I'll see you later?"

Brooks doesn't answer. Jo scoops up our empty glasses and heads back to the kitchen.

"What was that about?" I ask.

"Nothing. She's angry with me about," she pauses. "Stuff," she says eventually.

"Stuff, huh? I hate it when people are angry with you about 'stuff'," I say.

Brooks smiles. "Yeah. Me too." She checks her watch. "I should get going. I promised Ben I'd mow the lawn this afternoon. We're still on for tomorrow to go through your stuff?"

"For sure," I nod. "I hope my stuff is easier to deal with than your stuff." Brooks gives me a crooked grin and shakes her head. As we head in opposite directions, Brooks on her way home and me on my way to Dad and Julie's, I think about Brooks' reaction to Jo. It was almost as if Jo was being protective of Brooks. Maybe she's just an overprotective friend? If I hadn't stopped coming to Roper's years ago, maybe I'd be Brooks' overprotective friend. Then again, maybe I'm just reading too much into it.

Fourteen

Brooks

I should have asked Riley if I could go have a swim in her pool after I mowed. The one thing I don't like about Uncle Pete's place is that he refused to get a pool put in. I'm only two blocks from the beach, but it would be nice to just laze in a pool without having sand creep into your underwear. Thankfully, Uncle Pete does have air conditioning, and I'm just about to settle back into the lounge and go channel surfing on the TV when the door bell rings.

When I open the door, I almost slam it shut again. The only thing that stops me is that Jo's not by herself. She has what looks like the rest of the protest group.

My protest group. I stand in the doorway so she can't just push her way in. "What do you want?"

"We just want to talk," she says. I know her innocent act is all for show in front of everyone else, but I don't doubt for a minute that she'd have a go at me again if she got the chance.

"About?"

"The group," she says. "We," she sweeps her hand around to encompass the others, "would like to discuss a few things."

"Like?"

"Like, where we go from here."

"From where, Jo?" I ask. "We decided last time that it's all over and there's no point organising any more protests. It's not going to make a difference."

"No, you decided," Jo says, her voice rising. She takes a breath. I hide my smirk. I know she's finding it hard to hold it together and it's hard for me to resist the urge to poke the bear. "Look," she says. "Can we just come inside? It's freaking hot out here and we just want to talk, that's all."

I think about what would be the worst possible scenario if I let them in. Jo obviously wants control of the group, and to be honest, I don't really care anymore. I doubt there's anything they can do to change my mind, so I make a decision. "I don't think there's anything to discuss." I look over to the rest of the group. "If you guys want to keep the group going, fine. Just leave me out of it."

"But you're the one who knows everything about the project," Sam says. "You're the one who did all the research and dug up that info from your mum's computer."

"What's stopping you from doing your own bloody research?" I ask. I'm trying to keep my cool because, with the exception of Jo, I'm friends with the rest of them.

"Research isn't the point," Jo says. "You're the one with inside knowledge. We can use that."

"What inside knowledge are you talking about?"

Jo glances back to the others. Sam nods at her. She turns back to me and says, "Riley. If you could get Riley to get us some intel—"

My jaw clenches and I can feel the heat rising in my face. "You have to be kidding me? I'm not asking Riley to do anything."

"Brooks, please. Just hear us out." Jo grabs my arm but I pull away.

"No, Jo. If you want to take charge, go ahead. Just leave me out of it." I don't want to talk about it anymore, and Jo was right. It is bloody hot outside. "And stay away from Riley," I warn. I slam the door before she can reply, and go back inside.

I'm half-way back up the hallway when the doorbell rings again. "You have to be kidding me."

I fling open the door. "What part of— Mum."

"I can't believe you're still insisting on having anything to do with that group," she says before she even says hello to me.

I turn and walk back inside, knowing she'll follow me. I can't just send her away like I can with Jo and the rest of the group.

"The protest at the community meeting was one thing but sabotaging the barge? That's on a whole other level, Brooks. It's criminal. Do you want to go to jail?"

I spin around. "Wait. What? Someone sabotaged the barge?"

"As if you didn't know," Mum says. "For God's sake, can you just let this be?"

"I don't know anything about the barge." I know she doesn't believe me so I change the subject. "Is that what you came over here for? To chastise me for having a conscience?"

"A conscience? Brooks, it's all well and good standing up for your principles, but you need to learn when to let things go."

"Why? Does it make you look bad that your own daughter is against your pet project?"

"Brooks!"

"Look Mum, if you just came over here to get up me for something you obviously think I did, then I don't want to hear it."

Mum narrows her eyes and glares at me. "You're still my daughter, Brooks, and no matter what you think, I don't want to see you get into trouble."

"So what, you came over to do the 'Good Mother' thing? To try to put me on the straight and narrow?" I emphasise the word 'straight' with my fingers because I know it will get a rise out of her. This time she doesn't bite.

She just takes a deep breath and gets out the pointy finger she loves so much. "I'm warning you, Brooks. If you get caught doing anything else with that protest group, I'm not going to come bail you out."

"Fine. Whatever. Is that it? Have you finished?"

She sniffs. "Your father misses you. I was going to ask you over for dinner, but under the circumstances, I don't think it would be a very good idea."

"Whatever you think," I reply. "And Dad knows where I am. He's welcome around here any time." What I don't say is that she's not, but Mum gets the hint and turns around and walks out. After I hear the front door close, I yell into the air at everything and nothing. I take a deep breath and go over to the TV cabinet to find one of Ben's Xbox games to play so I can take out my revenge on some unsuspecting virtual enemy. The more frustration I can get out of my system on a computer game, the less Ben will have to listen to when he gets home.

Fifteen

Riley

I get up early the next morning, only to miss Dad again, so I decide to catch him at his office on the esplanade. By the time I get there, it's a little after eight, but he doesn't seem to be around. I jiggle the door but it's still locked. I peer through the glass to see if I can see any movement but the inside office door is closed too. I'm sure Dad's here somewhere; his car's in the driveway.

I'm trying to decide whether to wait for him or just go home when someone taps me on the shoulder. I turn to see an old lady holding a string bag full of groceries. "You after Scott Fisher?" she asks.

"Yeah. Have you seen him?"

"Pfft. Good luck getting in to see him. No time for anyone these days," she says.

"Do you know him?"

"Everyone knows him." The way she says it, I'm not sure that's a good thing.

"I'm actually his daughter, Riley."

"Oh." She purses her lips and looks me up and down, like she's sizing me up. She squints her eyes and leans in closer. And then all of a sudden, she smiles. "You look like your mother."

That throws me. "Do I?"

"It's that red hair of yours," the old lady says, pointing vaguely at my head. "Your mother had wild hair when she was your age too."

This has me intrigued. "Did you know her?"

She ignores my question. "Too good for your father, that one." She clicks her tongue. "Couldn't tell her though. And look what happened." I'm just about to say that the cancer had nothing to do with my dad, but again, she continues the conversation without me. "Never should have married," she says, shaking her head.

I'm about to ask her what she means by that when Dad steps around the corner, a coffee cup in his hand. "Riley." He looks surprised to see me. He sees the old lady and says, "Hello, Mrs Marsh."

"Scott," Mrs Marsh replies. I notice the hint of wariness in the way she says his name.

"What can I do for you?" Dad asks, directing the question to Mrs Marsh.

"Oh, nothing," she replies. "Just catching up with young Riley here. Telling her how much she looks like Amy."

Dad's eyes narrow but he says, "She does, doesn't she?" Before Mrs Marsh can say anything more, Dad says, "If you'll excuse us, Mrs Marsh, I have a very important appointment to keep with my daughter."

"Oh, yes, of course. Wouldn't want to take up any of your valuable time." She smiles sweetly, but there's a little bit of venom in her voice. "Lovely to see you again, Riley." She pats my arm and wanders away.

Dad unlocks the office door and I follow him inside and into his office. This one looks like he's never here. "Do you even work here?" I ask.

"Of course I do. Why do you ask?" He takes a sip of his coffee.

I glance around. "It just looks so tidy."

Dad laughs. "Trudy keeps the mess hidden away for me. I can't see clients in a messy office."

"I guess not."

"So," Dad says, sitting back in his big leather chair behind the desk. "This is a surprise. Is everything okay?"

"Everything's fine. I just thought since you were so busy, I'd come and see you." He looks a little uncomfortable for some reason. "That's okay isn't it?" I ask.

He smiles. "Of course it is. I'm just, really in the middle of things at the moment, that's all."

I stand up. "Sorry. I should've called first. I'll let you get back to work."

As I turn to walk away, Dad says, "Riley, wait. We can have a chat while I drink my coffee. I could use a break anyway."

"Are you sure?"

"Yeah. Why not?" I sit back down and he asks, "So, are you settling in okay? Julie tells me you've been spending some time with Jason."

"Yeah. Jason's been pretty good actually. He helped move all the boxes and furniture from the container yesterday."

"Did he?"

"Yeah. That's actually why I'm here. I was wondering if you wanted to go through them with me. Help me decide what to keep."

"I actually have to be in Townsville tonight for a meeting first thing in the morning," Dad says.

"Oh, well it can wait until you get back."

Dad shifts on his chair. "I don't know, Riles. That's yours and your mothers' stuff. I'm not sure whether I'd be the right one to go through it with you."

My heart sinks but I don't tell Dad. Instead I say, "That's okay. I can sort it."

"Julie could help," Dad suggests. "She's pretty good at that sort of thing."

"It's okay. Brooks is coming over this afternoon to help me get started."

Dad sits up a little straighter. "Brooks is? That's nice of her."

"She's got the day off, and she offered, and it'll be great for us to catch up. I can't believe she's still here. I thought she'd be long gone after she finished school."

Dad doesn't reply. "Do you remember when we were kids?" I ask. "We used to get into trouble, huh?"

"Some things never change," Dad says, and he doesn't smile, which means he's actually serious. I wonder what it is about Brooks that he doesn't like, so I call him out on it.

"Don't you want me to be friends with Brooks?" I ask.

Dad takes a breath and lets it out slowly. "It's not that, exactly. I'd just much prefer it if you'd hang out with Jason. Make friends with his friends. They're your age."

"What? Like Damo?"

Dad smiles. "Good point." He puts down his coffee cup and leans forward in his chair. "It's been a long time since you were here, Riles, and a lot has changed. People have changed and Brooks, well, she's not the same person you used to know."

"I've changed too," I reply. "Everyone changes, Dad. You've changed. You never used to be so busy and now you are."

Dad sighs. "Riley, that's just the way life is. Everyone has to make money somehow and I'm sorry I'm busy right now, but hopefully when all this is over, I can take some time off." Conveniently, his phone rings. He looks down at it, but doesn't answer it. "Look. I have to get going before it gets too late. There's a lot of stuff about this project that I really want to tell you about, but it's going to have to wait until I get back from Townsville." He stands up and drops his coffee cup into a bin beside the desk.

I stand up and follow him to the front door. As he unlocks it, he says, "I know you want to talk to me about your mum and I promise I'll find some time as soon as I get this project sorted, okay?"

"Fine," I say.

He holds the door open for me. "I'll see you when I get back."

"Whatever," I mumble as I walk away.

I'm halfway back to the house when Jason rides up beside me on his skateboard. "Hey," he says. "What are you up to?"

"Heading home to get started on the boxes," I reply. Jason must pick up on my mood, because he takes my arm and pulls me to a stop.

"What's up?" he asks.

"Has he always been this painful to talk to?" I ask.

"Who? Scott?"

I nod.

Jason shrugs. "Not really. Why?"

"I just get the feeling he's avoiding me," I reply. "Like, he says he wants to spend time with me, and then he gets a phone call and has to go to work. As soon as I bring up Mum, he fobs me off."

Jason picks up his skateboard, tucks it under his arm and starts walking. I fall into step beside him. "He's always been good with me," he says. "I guess he's just trying to get into a new routine with you here."

"I haven't seen him in nearly five years, Jason. Don't you think he should want to spend some time with me?"

"Yeah, of course," Jason replies. "You've just picked a bad time to come up here that's all."

"I had no choice." I say it a little harsher than I mean to.

Jason sighs. "I didn't mean it like that." We walk on in silence for a while and then Jason says, "Scott's saved my arse a lot of times. He's a good guy."

"Why? What have you ever done?"

"Well, despite what you may have heard, I'm actually a bit of a rebel."

"You? No way."

"Yes way," Jason says. "I'm only allowed to finish school next year because Scott's buying new sports uniforms for the football and soccer teams."

I stop dead. "Dad bribed the school to stop you from being expelled?"

"When you say it like that, it kinda sounds bad."

"That's because it kinda is," I say. "Does that incident have anything to do with why Brooks got expelled?"

Jason laughs. "Nope. That was all Brooks's doing."

"So what happened?"

Jason scratches at the side of his skateboard with his fingernail. "I forgot to take my Leatherman out of my bag and for some reason, that was the day the Principal decided to do a random bag search."

"What's a Leatherman?" I ask.

"It's a tool I use for fixing my skateboard," Jason replies. "Anyway, the Principal found it and apparently thought I'd brought a weapon to school, so he hauled me up to the office and was threatening to expel me."

"For leaving a tool in your bag?"

"Yeah, well, I was also on my third strike, and they have this three strikes and you're out policy."

"So why didn't you get expelled?"

Jason shrugs. "I was sent home and Scott drove straight back down from Townsville the same day. Interrupted an important meeting with investors. Next thing I knew, I was being suspended and that was it. I could've missed almost a whole year of school if it wasn't for Scott."

I shake my head in disbelief. "You're so lucky."

"Yeah," Jason says. "In hindsight, getting suspended three times in the first couple of months of school wasn't very smart."

"When was your last one?"

Jason thinks for a moment and replies, "End of March I think? I didn't put a foot wrong after that one though."

I stop dead. "In March?"

"Yeah," Jason nods. "Why?"

"That's when Mum got her final diagnosis." A million thoughts start running through my head right then, and the one thing that sticks is the fact that Dad interrupted an important meeting to come back to Roper's to stop Jason from getting expelled, but couldn't even call me back for a week about Mum's cancer. "I can't even—" I close my eyes and suck in a breath, trying to stop the anger that's rising in my chest.

"What's the matter?" Jason asks.

I turn on him, and even though it's not him I'm angry at, he's the one who's in front of me. "Dad interrupted his work to help you," I stab at the air in front of him with my finger. "But didn't do the same for me when I needed him."

"No, that's not what I meant," Jason says, his hands up to pacify me.

I take a breath and calm down a little, fully aware this isn't Jason's fault. "I know what you were trying to say. But don't you get it? He left Townsville to help you, but not me. He put you over me." Anger starts to bubble back up in my chest and I don't let Jason say anything more. I turn and storm towards the house.

"Riley, wait!" Jason calls after me but I don't stop. He's just confirmed everything I already knew about my dad.

Sixteen

Brooks

I pull into the driveway at home and switch off the scooter. I'm pretty sure Mum's not here because on Monday mornings, she has her book club at Mrs Hetherington's place before she goes into her office at the council chambers in town.

As I head down between the garage and the side of the house, I hear the old push mower spluttering to life. Bloody Dad. He's got his earmuffs on at least, not that it matters because he's already going deaf in one ear, and he jumps when I grab his sleeve. He pulls off his earmuffs and steps away from the mower so he can hear me. I still have to yell at him. "What are you doing?" I ask.

"What's it look like?" he shouts back. "There's rain predicted in the next few days and if I don't get it done now, I won't get it done for weeks." He turns back to the mower but I grab his arm again.

"Let me do it." As much as I hate mowing, I know how much pain he'll be in after pushing that old mower around the acre block.

Before he can say anything I step in front of him and grab the handle. "Go and do the whipper snipping," I say, knowing that he won't do the whipper snipping because he still hasn't gotten the whipper snipper fixed yet. He will, however, go and potter in the shed until I'm done with the mowing. Better me being exhausted than him making his knee worse.

He pulls a face but lets me do it. Before he leaves, he pushes the earmuffs onto my head and ruffles my hair. I hate it when he does that but I let him get away with it.

After two hours of pushing the old mower around the yard, my legs are burning. Dad's been out a couple of times with cold water but apart from that, he's left me in peace. He used to be so anal about yard work that it used to drive me nuts trying to help him. The first time I ever mowed, he came out the next day, when I was at school, and went back over it because I'd missed a few spots. He also chastised me all the time for not emptying the catcher early enough. "You're leaving big clumps of cut grass everywhere, Brooks. It looks untidy," he'd say. Now, thankfully, he lets me do it my way. Although my way is his way because now I do it out of habit.

One habit I do like though is the beer we have together after the yard work's been done.

"It's only a light," Dad says, handing me a clear bottle of a brand I don't recognise.

"Beer's beer," I say, taking a big first gulp and almost choking on the bubbles.

Dad stifles a laugh. "Not to me it's not. Your mother's hidden all my heavies. This is the only stuff she'll let me drink."

I read the label. It's not even a standard drink. "It doesn't really count as a proper drink," I say.

"Well, whatever. It's still beer, so don't tell your mother," he says as he takes a long drink.

"No way," I reply. Mum doesn't know it, but Dad's been letting me have a beer with him every now and then since I was fifteen. It would be one more thing for Mum to freak out about, so it's a closely guarded secret.

"You sticking around for a bit?" Dad asks. "I've got some corned meat on the stove. Should be ready in time for lunch."

"Can't. I promised Riley I'd help her go through her mum's things this afternoon."

Dad nods. "You two picking up where you left off, hey?"

"I guess so," I reply.

He takes a long drink, licks his lips and then says, "Just be careful."

"Why? What's wrong with Riley?"

"Nothing," he shrugs. "She's grieving, that's all. Lots of..." he pauses. "Lots of feelings." I have no idea what he's talking about because he's never been good at these sorts of talks. At least he tries, so I cut him some slack, because I know he's worrying about me, not Riley.

"Feelings, huh?"

"Mmm-hhmm," he says. When I don't say anything, he looks at me. "What?"

"Nothing. You're just so good at this deep and meaningful stuff."

He picks up the bottle top and tosses it at me. We both laugh and I say, "Don't worry about me, Dad. I know Riley's going through a rough spot. Maybe she could use a friend, you know?"

"Maybe," Dad says.

I lean back in my chair and we both drink in silence for a bit. I finish my beer and stand up. "I should get going. I just called in to pick up some more of my stuff."

Dad sighs. "More stuff? So you're not planning on coming home any time soon?" He's disappointed. I can tell by the tone in his voice. Mum's probably been on his back about me, and whatever else she's been finding to nag him about, since I've been gone. I feel guilty about that because for years it was me she was nagging and leaving Dad alone.

"I don't know, Dad," I say, which is the honest truth. "Uncle Pete's is closer to work, so it's just better for me at the moment."

"What happens after summer?" Dad asks. "You have to decide what you're doing about school next year."

"I don't know. I haven't decided."

"Don't leave it too long."

"I know. I just need a few weeks to think about things."

"As long as you do," he says.

"I have to get going." I pick up my empty bottle and the bottle tops and head inside.

Seventeen

Riley

Brooks is quieter than usual and I'm wondering if it has anything to do with Jo. I watch her as she cuts open a box and peers inside. "Looks like pots and pans and stuff," she says. "Want me to unpack it?"

"No. I don't need any of it. Put the whole box into the charity pile."

"Your choice," she says and carries the box over to the corner where all the charity stuff is being put. She comes back over to the pile of boxes and opens another one. I seal up the box I've got (it's more kitchen stuff) and lug it over to the charity pile. I walk over and stand next to Brooks.

"Is everything okay?"

"Fine," Brooks says. I don't believe her. She flips open the top of the box and we both peer inside. "Towels," Brooks says, and she digs down deeper. "Feels like it's all towels."

"Charity," I say.

"Don't you want to keep any of this stuff?" Brooks asks. "There's a whole house full here. You could use all this when you move out into your own place."

"I know. It's just old though."

"You're getting rid of it because it's old? What are you, a snob now? You just want brand new shiny stuff?" I know she's joking but there's an edge to her voice.

"You can have any of this stuff you want," I say. "If you want to store all these boxes, you can have them."

"I don't want them," Brooks snaps.

I put my hand on her arm. "Brooks, something's wrong. Do you want to talk about it?"

She sighs. "Just, stuff on my mind I guess."

"Stuff, huh? Does this 'stuff' have anything to do with the 'stuff' Jo's angry with you about?"

Brooks looks up at me, a slight smile on her face. "Some of it." She takes a deep breath. "You know what? It doesn't matter. I'm supposed to be here helping you. So, let's just get this organised for you, okay?"

"Are you sure?"

"Of course I am. Today is supposed to be all about you."

"I feel like it's been all about me for the last year. I think I'm a bit over it."

"Well, maybe today should be the last day all about you then. Tomorrow can be all about me."

I wish she'd tell me what's on her mind, like she used to, but I guess she'll tell me if it's important. "Just so you know, you can talk to me about anything."

She smiles at me. "I know." She carries the box of towels over to the charity pile and comes back to stand beside me.

I open the next box and discover Mum's photo albums. "Oh my God." I open the first one and flip through the pages. "Look at all these old photos." It must be one of Mum's from before I was born. I don't recognise any of the people or the names in it. Brooks picks up another one.

"Hey, this one's got your name on it." She carries it over to the lounge and I follow her. We sit down side-by-side, and Brooks starts flipping through the pages. The very first picture is of me, wrapped up in a blanket in a hospital crib. "This must be when you were just born," Brooks says.

She flips the page over, and there's a picture of me with Mum and Dad, big grins on their faces. I trace the picture with my finger and sniff back a tear. Brooks looks at me. "Okay?" she asks. I nod.

I flip the page over and Brooks bursts out laughing. There's a picture of me in a baby bath, a washer covering my lower half. "I can see your boobies," Brooks teases and throws her head back laughing. She puts on a baby voice. "Look how widdle and cute you are." She prods at my side with her finger.

"So embarrassing." I flip the page over. "I think we should go through your baby albums, to even the score."

"No way," Brooks says. "That would mean I'd have to ask my mother where they are and since I'm fighting with Mum at the moment, that won't be happening."

"Are you?" I look at her. Brooks rests the album on her lap.

"Yeah. We had a big argument yesterday afternoon."

"Is that why you're so tense?"

"I guess so," Brooks says. "She just makes me so frustrated."

"I know what you mean." I put my hand on her leg and she looks at it for a moment before she puts her hand on top of mine.

She smiles at me and then picks the album back up. "I want to see if there are any more embarrassing photos in here," she says. "They could come in handy for your eighteenth birthday."

I laugh. "Your eighteenth is first," I remind her. "So be careful what you wish for."

She grins at me. Before we can look at any more photos, Brooks' phone rings. "Hey, Gloria," she says. "Tonight? I'll be up for that. Okay. I'll see you then." She hangs up and says, "How would you like to help me do takeaway deliveries tonight?"

I glance at the pile of unopened boxes strewn around the place. I could definitely use a break from it all. "I am so up for that."

Brooks stands up. "I should get home and have a quick shower. I'll be back in an hour to pick you up. And then after we're finished, we can go through those photo albums again."

"Oh, I'll be hiding those albums after you leave."

Brooks laughs as she closes the door behind her.

I don't feel like going through any more boxes, so I sit on my bed and look through the photo albums. The early ones of me when I was a baby, when Mum and Dad are still together, make me a little heart sick. I wonder what my life would've been like if we'd stayed at Roper's instead of moving away after the divorce. Would Brooks and I still be friends? Would Dad have become a developer, or would he have just been happy building other people's houses? Would Mum have gotten cancer? I know that's a stupid thought, and I guess it doesn't matter now anyway.

I flip the pages and the photos change to ones of me on holidays with Dad. In most of the early ones, he's wearing really long board shorts and I'm in frilly little-girl togs and we're both grinning at the camera. Dad's hair is down to his shoulders and he's even got abs. I can see what Mum saw in him back then. Back when he must have been fun.

A few more pages and I get a bit older, maybe around seven or eight, and Brooks starts appearing in them. There's one of us riding our bikes along the esplanade, just after the footpath was built. There's another one of us at her Uncle Pete's house, me standing on a kitchen chair to reach the pool table and Brooks peering over the edge, watching me. I can't help but smile. Things were so easy back then. Mum didn't have cancer and the summer holidays were my favourite time of year.

I flip over to the next page and something drops out onto my lap. It's an old, yellowing envelope addressed to me. It's been opened. I can't read the return address on the back because the flap is torn up. Inside is a small piece of paper, folded in half and when I open it, I feel like I've been punched in the gut. Inside is a blue and red friendship bracelet; Brooks and my favourite colours. I immediately realise the significance of Brooks' tattoo. I open the letter, excited to see what it says.

Dear Riley

I didn't know whether you would still have your bracelet or not, so I made you another one. I hope you get it. I still have mine. I wear it everywhere. Even in the shower. I just wanted you to know that I miss you, and wish you would write to me and tell me why you haven't come back. I wanted to ask your dad but Mum told me to mind my own business. As if you aren't my business. I hope you're okay and I hope you come back soon. (Or write to me.)

Love always from your best summer friend forever,
Brooks

There's no date on the letter, so I have no idea when Brooks wrote it. One thing's for sure, I never got it. If I had, I would've written back to Brooks and told her why I didn't come back. I would've told her that no matter how much I wanted to come and see her, I just couldn't because Dad didn't have any time for me. I would've worn the bracelet too. I don't know why Mum would have hidden the letter from me. I wish I could ask her. Maybe if I'd gotten Brooks' letter, I might've made the effort with Dad and visited him again.

I turn the bracelet over in my hand, remembering back to the day Brooks and I sat cross-legged under the camphor laurel tree in the caravan park, weaving together some scraps of wool we found when we cleaned out one of the cabins. I don't remember exactly what we said when we tied them on each others' wrists but it probably would've been 'friends forever', or something like that.

I realise too, that our friendship must've meant a lot to Brooks if she chose to get our friendship bracelet tattooed on her wrist. For some reason, that thought makes me tingle inside. I can't wait to show her the letter and the bracelet when she gets back.

Eighteen

Brooks

Riley and I have so far delivered a ham and pineapple pizza to the Jameson's, fish and chips to a family at the caravan park, and a big box of stuff from the hot box to the Sea Breeze Motel where some of Scott Fisher's construction crew are staying. Sam's beeped and waved at us from his little Suzuki van a couple of times as we've passed each other on our way out or back to the Hut. He was roped into doing deliveries too, just for tonight to see how we all went.

It's been busier than usual for a Monday night which is good for Gloria and Stav, and the weather's cooler which means I'm not sweating as much as I normally would be with Riley hugging into my back on the scooter. There's a storm off the coast looking like it might roll in later on, which explains the cool change and the breeze picking up.

After we drop off our last delivery, (the Katsidis brothers obviously didn't catch anything today judging by the eight pizzas they ordered), I park the scooter at the back of the Hut. We're hoping we get to pick over the hot box before Gloria turfs out what's left. Riley pulls off her helmet and shakes out her hair. I almost laugh because it looks like one of those shampoo commercials.

"What?" she asks.

"Nothing," I reply, and lead her inside through the back door. Ben pulls me aside as I head past the fryers.

"Hey," he says. "Think you can make yourself scarce at home?"

"Why?"

He takes a quick look behind him. "Nicki's coming over," he whispers.

"To go over the new menu?" I ask, wiggling my eyebrows.

"Funny," he says. "You're a comedian."

"What do you want me to do? Lock myself in my room?"

"No. Just, can't you find something else to do? Just for a couple of hours."

I smirk.

"We're just watching a movie, Brooks. Please, can you just not be there?"

I decide to stop joking around and let him off the hook. "Yeah, fine. Riley and I have some crap food to eat so we'll find somewhere else to eat it."

"Thanks," he says.

"You owe me one," I say to his back. He gives me the finger over his shoulder without even turning around. I laugh it off and head out to the front of the shop to see what fried food is left.

Back outside, with a box full of chicken wings, potato scallops, chips and a chicko roll (which I've called dibs on), I say to Riley, "Did you want to go to the park or something? Stay out a bit later?"

The breeze picks up and whips Riley's hair across her face as she tries to put on her helmet, and there's a rumble of thunder in the distance. "That storm's a bit close, don't you think?" she asks.

I shrug. "It's a while away yet."

She doesn't look convinced, and I do remember how much she hates storms. "Ben's asked me to give him and Nicki some privacy, so we can't go back to my place."

"We could go back to mine. I do practically have a whole little house to myself."

I nod. "Great idea, Riles."

Riley swings onto the bike behind me, takes the box of food and we head off.

As I ride the bike up the driveway, Riley points to the back patio. I pull up beside it, and she gets off. "Put it under there," she says. "It'll be protected from the storm."

"It'll be fine. It'll just be a bit of rain."

I follow Riley across the patio and to the back door of the house. She sticks her head inside and says, "Hey, Jason. Are Dad and Julie home?"

Jason comes over to the back door. "Julie's in bed and Scott's in the study. Do you want me to get them?"

"No," Riley replies. "Just wanted to let them know I'm home, that's all."

"No worries." He sniffs the air. "What's in the box?"

Riley flips open the lid and Jason peers inside. He goes to take the Chiko roll but I grab his hand. "I called dibs," I say. He looks up and grins.

"Take whatever else you want though," Riley says.

He digs into the box and takes a handful of chips and a potato scallop. "Thanks."

"We're going to wait out the storm in the guest house," Riley says. "You can come hang out if you like."

"Nah. I'm kicking Damo's arse in Halo. I'll see you in the morning."

He turns and shuts the door, and Riley and I head over to her place.

By the time we've stuffed ourselves full of fried food, the storm has well and truly hit. I've successfully managed to not tell Riley about Jo or my mother, and thankfully, she's not pushed me. It's not that I don't want to tell her about that stuff, because I would, normally. It's just that she's had such a rough few months that she doesn't need to hear me bitching about my mother, who is alive and kicking when her mother isn't.

We're spread out on the floor in front of the lounge, flipping through a folder full of Riley's school report cards and random pieces of artwork, when Riley jumps up. "You'll never guess what I found today," she says excitedly. She takes something from the drawer in her bedside table and sits back down beside me. "Close your eyes and hold out your hands."

I do as I'm told and when Riley tells me to open my eyes, I can't believe what I'm seeing. "You're kidding me?" I turn the bracelet over in my hand. "Where did you find it?"

"It was in one of the photo albums," she replies. "Can you believe it's lasted so long?"

"No. I can't."

She touches my tattoo with her finger. "That's what this is, isn't it?"

"Yeah."

"Why did you pick that?" she asks.

I could say it's because I never wanted to forget her, but I know she'd freak out, so I say, "It reminds me how happy I was when I was little."

"It must've meant a lot to you," Riley says, tracing the outline of the tattoo with her finger.

"You did," I reply without even thinking.

A smile spreads across Riley's face. "There's something else," she says, dropping a small envelope into my hand.

My breath catches in my throat and I swallow hard. I know exactly what it is. Before I can say anything, Riley says, "I never got it, Brooks. I didn't even know you wrote to me."

I let out a breath and open the letter. It's bittersweet reading the words, and even now I can remember how much I missed her back then. The bracelet was my last ditch effort to get her to write to me. "This was the last one I wrote," I say, staring at my twelve-year-old scrawl.

"Last one? There were more?"

I nod slowly. "Heaps."

Riley takes my hand and squeezes. "I'm so sorry. I never even knew."

"It's okay. Really." I glance up at her and if there was any bit of anger left for her not writing back, and for her leaving Roper's and not coming back, it's gone now. I smile back at her and we stay like that for what seems like ages.

A huge crack of thunder booms outside, and Riley jumps. Instinctively, I put my arm around her shoulder. "It's just a storm, Riles." The wind howls and the rain starts bucketing down again. The lights flicker off and Riley whimpers. When they come back on, she's got her eyes squished shut and she's sucking in short, sharp breaths. I have to think of a way to stop her from panicking. I glance around the room and my gaze settles on the piles of boxes that are meant to be going to charity. They give me an idea.

"Hey, Riles. Remember what we used to do at Uncle Pete's during the storms?"

Riley opens her eyes and looks at me. "Hide under the pool table?"

"Exactly," I reply.

She looks over at the dining table pushed up against the wall. "We can't fit under there."

"We're not going to hide under the table. Just give me a minute, okay?" I jump up off the floor and head over to the bed. "Mind if I take the sheet off?"

Riley shakes her head. Thunder booms again and she squeals. I pull the top sheet from the bed and head over to the boxes. I take the smaller ones off the top and then pull the bigger ones forward.

Eventually, after moving them around like a Tetris game, I've created a U-shaped space. I race back over to the bed and grab the pillows, and the cushions from the lounge chair as well. I lay them out on the floor between the boxes, and then I drape the sheet over the whole thing, stacking the smaller boxes back on top to stop it from slipping off. I turn back to Riley. "Ta da!"

"You made a fort." She tries to smile but I can see how hard she's trying not to panic.

"Uh-huh. Do you want to come and check it out?"

She jumps up and comes over to stand beside me. I sweep aside the sheet so she can duck under and crawl inside. She crawls right to the back, turns around and sits, cross-legged on the cushions.

"Comfy," she says. "Are you coming in?"

"Of course." I crawl in and sit beside her. It's smaller than I thought, so we're a little squished. Our sides are touching from our shoulders down to our hips. I stretch my legs out so my feet are sticking out from the sheet. Riley does the same thing and she nudges my leg with hers. When I look at her, she's smiling, just a little. "Thanks," she says. "I really, really hate storms."

Thunder rolls around outside again and she shudders. I take her hand in mine. "The storms are quick up here. It won't take long to go over."

She swallows and nods her head. "We're safe in here, right?"

"Rols. We're in a fort. Of course we're safe."

"I haven't heard anyone call me that for ages," Riley says. "You used to call me that when I was angry at you, remember? Or when you wanted to get my attention?"

"Yeah." I nod. "It wasn't a very good nickname. Sorry."

"It's okay. I actually don't mind it now." She gives me a half smile and just when I think she's doing okay, a loud crack reverberates through the air. It even makes me jump. Something crashes down outside and Riley screams. She starts hyperventilating. "We're going to die. We're going to die," she says, over and over again.

"Riley, it's okay. We're safe." She's not listening to me, so I turn her head to me and when I see the terror in her eyes, I do the only thing I can think of to calm her down. I kiss her.

Nineteen

Riley

Mum told me once that the first time she kissed my dad, her world just melted away and she felt like there was just the two of them. I was totally grossed out at the time at the thought of them kissing that passionately, but I have to say that I can now totally understand what Mum meant.

It's not that I haven't kissed anyone before, because I have. And it's not that I haven't ever thought about kissing Brooks either, because I've done that too. I mean, I wanted to kiss her yesterday on the beach, but that would have been really embarrassing, and I wanted to kiss her this afternoon when she was upset, but it just didn't feel like the time. I just never thought I'd be kissing her in a box fort in a storm. Totally new situation for me. A totally new and wonderful situation that pushes the storm to the back of my mind, at least for the moment.

Her hand moves to my hip and I feel her fingers squeeze my skin. Before I know it, my hand is on the back of her neck, pulling her into me. Her lips are soft and warm against mine and a little salty from the fried food we ate earlier. She tilts her head slightly and touches my lips with her tongue. I don't mean to, but I shiver.

Brooks pulls away from me and looks down at her lap. "Sorry," she mumbles.

"Totally fine," I whisper. "Totally."

"Are you sure?" she asks.

I bite my lip and nod. "Made me forget the storm." Thunder cracks overhead. "At least for a minute." I lay my head on Brooks' shoulder and we reposition ourselves so she can put both arms around me and hug me.

She kisses the top of my head. "It'll be over soon."

We lay like that for a while, listening to the rain drumming down outside and every time the lightning and thunder pulses through the sky, Brooks hugs me tighter.

"Mum loved storms," I say.

"Did she?"

"Yeah. She used to run outside in the rain and get soaking wet." I smile at the memory of my mother jumping in puddles and trying to coax me outside to dance around with her. I feel a twinge of sadness that I didn't do it more often. Maybe I wouldn't be so afraid of storms now if I did.

"Tell me about your mum," Brooks says.

"What do you want to know?"

"I don't know. Tell me anything you can think of. Like, did she ever tell you how she met your dad?"

"At work," I say.

"They worked together?" Brooks asks.

"Not really. Mum was a copy writer and she used to write Dad's sales ads for him for the display houses he built."

"Wow. Really? Was she good at it?"

"I guess so. It's what she did for a job back home until she got sick."

Brooks squeezes my hand. "I bet she was really good with words."

"Yeah. She was great when I had assignments to do."

Brooks chuckles. "I wish I had your mum when I was doing mine."

I smile. "She was great at seeing the best in things too, you know? Like, a two-bedroom tiny house was a cosy cottage, or a main road was easy access to transport."

Thunder booms again and I suck in a breath and tense up. Brooks squeezes my leg.

"What about people?" she asks.

"What do you mean?"

"Well, if your mum was trying to sell Ben, for example. What would she say?"

I like how Brooks is talking like Mum's still here, instead of in the past like everyone else does. I think about Ben on the beach yesterday, how chiselled his body is and how Nicki fawned over him. "She'd say he has good street appeal."

Brooks cracks up laughing.

"What?" I ask.

"Nothing. Sorry. What else would she say?"

"Um, chef's kitchen?"

Brooks nods her approval. "Good one."

"And maybe good for entertaining?"

Brooks laughs again. "I think you've nailed it. Wait til I tell him." She leans her head on mine and runs her finger down my arm. "What about me?"

"You?"

"Why not? What would your mum say about me if I was a house?"

I glance up at her, and the way she's looking at me, all soft and mellow, makes my skin tingle. I realise all of a sudden how little I know about her now, so I take a guess. "Rough around the edges," I say. Brooks raises her eyebrows but says nothing, so I continue. "Inside is deceptively big. Discerning buyers only. Price on application."

Brooks slaps her thigh and throws her head back and laughs. "Price on application. I love it. What about you?"

"Me?"

"Is there an echo in here? Yes, you." She taps me on my nose with her finger.

I sit up and pull away from her, as much as I can in our current situation anyway. "I don't know."

"Yes, you do," Brooks presses. "What type of house is Riley?"

I pick at my nails and Brooks takes my hand and squeezes. "Come on," she says. "How would you get me to buy you?"

Her question makes me laugh. I take a deep breath. "Lacking street appeal. Waiting for the right owner. Serious buyers only." I look back up at her, waiting for her reaction. Her expression has gotten serious.

She chews on her lip. "You know what I'd say?"

I shake my head.

"Classic Queenslander. Could do with some TLC. Knock down some walls to really open up."

I know she's trying to be funny, but I don't think she has any idea how close she actually is about me. For some reason, hearing Brooks say that makes me tear up. I sniff.

"Oh, Rols. I didn't mean to make you cry."

"No, I'm not." I wipe my eyes with my shirt. "Sorry."

Brooks pulls me in closer and wraps me in a tight hug. "I'm sorry, Rols. We don't have to talk about your mum anymore." Her mouth is just above my ear and when she talks, her breath is warm on my skin.

"It's okay. Really. I just miss her, you know?"

"Yeah. I know."

I lean into her more and her arms tighten around me again. Thunder booms overhead but it's not as loud as before. I close my eyes against it and just try to think about how good it feels to be with Brooks. The sweet smell of soap on her neck and the tang of whatever product she uses in her hair.

Brooks jumps up all of a sudden and hits her head on the sheet ceiling. I laugh. "What are you doing?"

She drops back down onto her knees, grabs my hand and pulls me up. "Come on," she says, pulling me out of the fort and toward the door.

"Where are we going?"

"Outside," she says.

I freeze. "Wait. What? It's storming out there."

She stops, her hand on the door handle, and turns to look at me. "Rols, it's just raining now. The storm's gone. Haven't you noticed the thunder's not so loud anymore?"

"I don't care. I'm not going out there."

Brooks sighs. She takes a step toward me, and takes both my hands in hers. She looks me in the eyes. She's so intense. "Riley Fisher, it's raining outside, and you just told me that your mum used to love dancing in the rain. Don't you want to see why she loved it so much?"

I chew on the inside of my mouth. She's not being fair and I reckon she knows it.

"Come on, Rols. I promise I won't let anything happen to you."

"We'll catch a cold."

"It's still at least thirty degrees out there," Brooks counters.

"We'll get wet, and you don't have any spare clothes."

"I'll borrow some of yours."

"It's almost eleven at night."

"I still don't see your point."

I don't move.

Brooks lowers her voice, so it's almost a whisper. "Come on, Rols. Just come outside for five minutes and if you hate it, we can come back in." She takes a step back, and pulls me a step forward. She slides the door open behind her. "See? It's not even windy anymore." She smiles at me and the way she looks at me, her eyes soft, one eyebrow raised, the corners of her mouth turned up just a touch, it makes my stomach flip. I give in and let her lead me outside and into the rain.

The rain is now more like a shower, and by the time we walk around the side of the pool and onto the grass at the back, we're both soaked through. She turns to face me and walks backwards. "Okay?" she asks. I nod.

We stop in the middle of the yard. "Not so bad, huh?"

I shake my head. "What do we do now?"

"We dance," Brooks says, and starts swinging my arms and jumping around.

"There's no music," I say.

"It's in your head. Remember what your mum used to do? Do that."

I close my eyes and lift my head to the sky, feeling the rain on my face, and I picture Mum the last time I saw her dancing in the rain and I start to move. I see her laughing and twirling in front of me, the long dark hair of her favourite wig sticking to her face. Reaching out for me trying to coax me out with her, and I start to cry. My tears mix with the rain falling down my cheeks and I forget the storm. It's just me and Mum, dancing in the rain like I should have so many times.

I open my eyes. Brooks has stopped dancing. She's standing there, soaking wet, watching me intently. I smile at her and she smiles back at me and my breath catches in my throat. I step over to her and press my lips onto hers, and she kisses me back. And we stand there in the rain, dripping wet, in the blue glow from the pool, and it's amazing.

Twenty

Brooks

My alarm jolts me awake the next morning and I fumble around on the floor under Riley's bed trying to find my phone before she wakes up. I finally manage to turn the alarm off, but not before Riley groans and stretches beside me.

"What time is it?" she asks groggily.

"Too early for you. Go back to sleep." I lean over and kiss her on the cheek and then duck into the bathroom to get changed out of the shorts and shirt I borrowed from her last night and back into my own clothes.

When I come back out, Riley's splayed across the bed on her stomach like a star fish and has clearly fallen straight back to sleep. I stand for a moment, watching her slow steady breaths, her hair a mess over the pillows. She looks so cute in her Hello Kitty pyjamas. I wish I could climb back into bed with her and snuggle again but I have to get home and get ready for work, and with any luck, I'll get back before Ben wakes up and can give me shit for staying out all night. Although I can't wait to hear how his night went.

Sneaking into Uncle Pete's has never been easy, thanks to the squeaky front door. If you open it slowly, it squeaks loud enough to wake the whole house up, but if you open it fast, it doesn't squeak at all. Turns out it doesn't matter either way, because when I get to the kitchen, Ben's already up and cooking breakfast.

He looks up and before he can even open his mouth I say, "I waited out the storm at Riley's place and I fell asleep, so it was just easier to stay."

"Right," he says. He dumps whatever he's been mixing from a bowl into a pan.

"What's for breakfast?" I ask.

Ben sprinkles herbs into the pan. "This is not for you."

"A cooked breakfast. That's unusual." And then it hits me. "Oh my God. Ben!"

He glances over to the hallway. "Shh," he says. "You'll wake her up."

"No wonder you didn't call or text me last night. You were too busy."

He points a wooden spoon at me. "Like you can talk."

"Hey," I say, putting my hands up. "Riley and I fell asleep waiting out the storm. You on the other hand—"

He cuts me off. "I, on the other hand, slept on the lounge."

"You did not."

"Take a look if you don't believe me." He points to the lounge room, so I wander over and take a look. Sure enough, there are blankets and pillows on the lounge, and it does look like someone might have slept there.

"Are you sure you didn't just do that for my benefit?" I ask, wandering over to the pantry to get my cereal.

Ben just smiles at me. "How about we call it even. You just fell asleep with Riley and I slept on the lounge."

"Okay then," I reply, but I'm still not sure he believes me. Which means maybe I shouldn't believe him.

I sit at the breakfast bar and watch him cook. I do the same thing at the Hut sometimes when they're not busy and Ben's on the grill. His hands are so fast, cutting stuff up and then tossing it into the pan. He's making an omelette. Pretty easy to make (even I can make them) but pretty spectacular when you're trying to impress someone if you do it right. I watch as he tosses spinach and tomatoes on top and then sprinkles cheese on right at the last minute. Then he eases the omelette across the pan and flicks the corner up so that it folds over on itself. He looks up at me and grins. He used to practice that for ages until he got it just right.

"Show off." I laugh and finish off my cereal. "I have to get ready for work," I say, dumping my bowl into the sink. "I'll catch you tonight, and you can tell me all the goss."

"Looking forward to all your goss," he says with a wink.

Work is quiet so I spend most of my time unpacking the new boxes of stock and daydreaming about where I should take Riley on a date. I mean, here's the thing. Riley and I used to sleep in the same bed when we were kids all the time. It's just something you do when you're little, right? And I know we kissed last night, but that could have just been Riley freaking out from the storm and not realising what she was doing. There was that kiss in the rain that she instigated. I smile at the memory of that one. But still, I need to find out whether Riley will kiss me under normal circumstances, like when there's no storm around.

The other problem is, I have no idea whether Riley's 'out' or not. I mean, everyone knows I'm out. If they didn't before then the rainbow flag incident at school a few months ago made sure of it. But Riley? I have no idea if she's out to herself let alone anyone else, so I need to be careful, just in case. Roper's is such a small town, and I am well aware of what some people think of me, and I'd hate for Riley to be associated with the bad me.

And then there's her dad, who I'm sure would freak out completely if he found out about me and Riley last night. I'm not exactly his favourite person at the moment. He may have won the development war, but I caused him a few wounds in the battle and although my protesting days are over, I doubt he'll forgive me too easily for causing him so much trouble.

I'm racking my brain trying to come up with a place to take Riley, or something to do which is kind of a date but could be taken either way when Reece comes out the back and says, "You've got a visitor."

I jump up and grin.

"What are you so happy about?" he asks as I rush past him.

"Nothing," I reply and head over to the counter, where it's not Riley who's popped in, but Rosie. I try to hide my disappointment. "Hey, Rosie. What's up?"

"Hey, Brooks. I just came in to see if you wanted to give me a hand tonight."

"Oh yeah. For sure. Did we get any in last night?"

"No. I think the storm kept them away. We'll see how we go tonight though."

"What time do you want me over there?"

"Around nine. I'm heading over early so I'll meet you over there. Usual spot."

"Great," I reply. "Oh, hey. Can I bring a friend?"

Rosie shrugs. "Sure. The more the merrier." She smiles and waves. "See you later."

"See you." I wave back and watch her weave her way around the clothes racks. I need to call Riley and make sure she's okay with being out so late, and I realise that I don't actually have her phone number. I wonder if Reece talked Riley into a loyalty card last week? I log into the computer at the counter and drill own into the customer database. Sure enough, Riley's details are there. I don't want to think about whether Reece got these details for himself. I'm just glad he got them.

Now I know it's against company policy to access customer details for our own personal gain, and I also know that every keystroke we do is recorded, so I tag Riley's customer card with a note that says I'm calling her to follow up on a question she had about new stock coming in, and then I write her phone number down on a piece of paper and head out the back to the stock room.

I dig my phone out of my backpack and take a deep breath before I punch in her number. For some reason my mouth has gone dry. It rings and rings and then just as I'm about to hang up, it goes to her message bank. I close my eyes as I listen to Riley's voice telling me to leave a message and then when it beeps, just in case Reece is listening in, I say, "Hey, Riley. It's just Brooks from The Surf Shop. Can you call me back when you get the chance? On this number would be great. Thanks. Bye."

I hang up, and smile to myself. I'll bet no-one's ever taken Riley on a date like I'm going to tonight.

Twenty-one

Riley

It's mid-morning by the time I get out of bed, and the only reason I get up in the first place is because Jason comes in to wake me up to see if I want to go paddle boarding with him. When he sees the remnants of the box fort Brooks made last night, he says, "Do I want to know why you built a fort?"

"Safety from the storm," I reply. I'm impressed that he actually recognises what it is. He doesn't ask any more questions, thankfully.

He just says, "I'm heading down to the beach in an hour or so, so if you wanted to, I could teach you how to paddle board."

"Actually, that sounds pretty good. Just let me get changed and have something to eat."

"Sure," he shrugs. "I'll see you inside."

After he's gone, I do a quick tidy up before I head to the bathroom to have a shower. The place looks like a bomb's hit it.

Jason's making coffee when I get over to the house.

"Where's Julie?" I ask.

"She's off on some meditation retreat. She left this morning."

"Oh. Is Dad at the office today? I was going to go and see him, since I keep missing him at home."

"He's working from home, actually," Jason says. "He's in the study. You should go see him. He asked about you at breakfast this morning."

"He did?" I wonder whether he mentioned our argument.

"Yeah. I think he wants to take you over to the island to show you the site."

I start to head down the hall and Jason says, "You should take him this." He holds up a coffee mug. "He'll be ready for another one."

"Thanks." I take the coffee and head down the hall.

The door to the study is open, which I take as a sign that Dad's not overly busy, so I knock on the door and then step inside. Dad's office is pretty sparse but there's paperwork and folders piled up on every available bit of floor. He has a desk that looks out over the garden at the side of the house, and there's a bookcase in one corner and two-seater lounge on the opposite wall to the desk. Apart from that, there are pictures of houses and house plans all over the walls. I guess this is where he does most of his work judging by the mess.

He turns when I come in and smiles at me. He's got his phone to his ear and he holds up his finger and mouths "Just a sec." I nod and take a seat on the lounge.

"Just get it sorted," he says into the phone and hangs up. He walks over and sits on the lounge beside me. "Hey, Riles. You look like you're in a good mood. Did you have a good night last night?"

I hand him the cup. "Yeah. Brooks and I stayed up late catching up."

He nods and sips his coffee. "Riles, I'm sorry about our argument."

"It's okay," I reply. "I know you've got a lot of stuff on your mind."

"It's not okay," Dad says. "I'm just trying to sort out some last minute stuff with the development, but that's no excuse for getting upset with you for no reason."

I look down at my hands and shrug.

He twists the mug in his hand. "I'm sorry about your mum, Riles. And I'm sorry I haven't been around."

I don't say anything because I'm not sure what he wants me to say. I want to say it's okay, even though it's really not, because I don't want to make him feel worse than he obviously is. He continues. "Once all this stuff is over, the development stuff, we'll sit down and have a good talk, yeah?" His phone rings and I can see he wants to answer it.

"It's okay, Dad. I know you're busy."

He lets the phone ring out, and since I don't really want to talk to him about Mum right now, I change the subject. "Jason said you wanted to take me over to the island to show me the site."

Dad brightens. "Yeah, I do." His phone rings again and he sighs. "I just have all of this stuff to sort out and then we can organise a time."

"What sort of stuff?" I ask. Everyone seems to be having problems with 'stuff' at the moment.

"Well," he says. "That storm last night was pretty fierce. It took down a couple of big branches on some of the trees on the island. The contractors have a bit of cleaning up to do before the Minister gets here next week."

"Will it be ready?"

"Yeah. If it's not, we'll just take her to somewhere that looks tidier. The site's pretty big so it doesn't really matter where we do the official stuff. It's all for show anyway." He takes another sip of coffee. "What are you up to today?"

"Jason's going to take me paddle boarding."

"Really? Have you done it before?"

"No. He's going to teach me. Is it hard?"

Dad shrugs. "It's a little tricky to start off with, but the water's flat most of the time, so you shouldn't have any trouble picking it up."

"Jason said he goes with you in the mornings."

Dad relaxes back into the lounge. "Yeah, most mornings I try to get out there. You should come with us, if you can get out of bed early enough." He nudges my shoulder with his.

"Why don't you come with us today?"

"Oh," he says, looking back at his desk. "I have a few things I need to get done today." He looks back at me. "I'll try to get it all done today so we can go out in the morning. Is that okay?"

"I guess so." I stand up. "I should get going. I have to have some breakfast before I go."

"Don't you mean lunch?"

"I just got up. I haven't had breakfast yet."

"Fair enough," Dad says. He smiles. "I should get back to it. I'll see you later, hey?"

"Yeah." I head back out to the kitchen.

After falling off three times before I even get going, making Jason crack up laughing, I finally manage to stand on the paddle board and do a few tentative strokes.

"Stand up straighter," Jason calls to me. He's way out in the deeper water, while I'm still paddling around where I can at least touch the bottom if I fall off again. I rock a little as I reset my footing and I stand up straight, just like he's told me and after a few more rows, I think I'm finally getting the hang of it.

"Paddle like this and you'll turn towards me," Jason calls. I watch him as he pushes the paddle further away from the board and turns to face me. I do the same thing, and what do you know, I slowly turn the board to face him. He paddles over so he's closer to me and doesn't have to yell. "You're doing great," he says, grinning at me. "Want to go a little deeper out?"

I'm feeling a little braver, so I say, "Yeah. Why not?"

Jason turns his board around and I follow him as he paddles out into deeper water. I'm slow at first, while Jason shoots ahead, with his long deliberate strokes. He slows down further out and turns to wait for me. When I get to him we follow the shoreline for a bit and then Jason suggests we have a break. As we're making our way back to the beach, Jason says, "Look who's come down."

I look up to see Dad in his rashie and board shorts, his board under his arm. When we get to the beach, we drag our boards up onto the sand and grab a cold drink from the soft cooler we brought down. Dad sits down beside us on the sand.

"I thought you had a heap of work to do?" I ask.

"Well, I wanted to show you the development before work got started, and I need to go across to have a look at the damage from the storm last night, so I thought I'd kill two birds with one stone."

"You want me to paddle all the way across to the island?" I ask.

"It's not that far," Jason says. "We do it all the time."

"Easy for you. You've been doing this for years," I reply.

"You were doing great out there, Riles," Dad says. "You shouldn't have any problems getting across. The water's flat and there's hardly any breeze so it'll be a cinch."

I'm glad Dad's come down to the beach to paddle board with us. I'm a bit iffy about being able to get over to the island and back without falling off at least once, or getting sore arms, but the fact that Dad's taken the afternoon off means a lot. "Okay. Let's do it."

Dad smiles and gives me a one-armed hug. As we head down to the water, Dad says, "Did you tell Mrs Harper your mother got hit by a car?"

I glance up at him and he doesn't seem angry, so I say, "Maybe."

He shakes his head. "Why on earth would you do something like that, Riles?"

We lay our boards in the water and apparently that wasn't a rhetorical question, because he lays his hand on my board, preventing me from pushing off.

"Because," I say. "I was just sick of the sympathy over Mum's cancer."

Dad doesn't say anything and I get the feeling it's not really the answer he's looking for. I sigh. "Your mum dies of cancer, people want to tell you about their aunt or their mother or their grandmother or whatever, and how they had cancer too. And I have to relive it all again while they tell me all about what they went through. You tell them your mum got hit by a car, and they just go away."

Dad considers this and finally he says, "I get it. Just don't go saying that to anyone else, okay?" He smiles at me.

"Okay," I reply.

As we push off on our boards, Dad says, "I'll race you." Before I can even stand up on my board, he and Jason are off. I finally feel like I might be a part of this family.

Twenty-two

Brooks

Riley didn't call me back until late afternoon, by which time I was panicking, thinking she was totally freaking out about what had happened last night. Thankfully she was just busy with Scott and Jason most of the day. I haven't exactly told her what we're doing tonight, so I'm a little surprised she's actually happy to come with me, especially when I told her it would be another late night.

"I can't believe you slept so late," I say as I lead her down to the beach.

"I can't believe you came to get me wearing a head torch," Riley replies. "What are we doing? Digging to China?"

"I told you, all will be revealed soon enough."

She wraps her arm around mine and pulls me to her. It's nice being so close to her again. I scan the beach every now and then until I find where I put the canoe. When we get to it, Riley asks, "Are you taking me to the island?"

"Yes, I am." I take Riley's backpack from her and place it with mine in the middle of the canoe. "Hop in."

She does as she's told and I push us off and jump in. The moon is still low behind the trees on the island, but it's bright enough to navigate by so I turn my head torch off. Gliding across the water this late at night, when you're not moving, it's so quiet, your ears ring. But when you're paddling, the water lapping against the hull with each stroke is like little explosions going off on the side.

"Do you have any idea how romantic this is?" Riley asks from her position up front.

"I have some idea," I reply. She turns to me but I can't see her expression because her face is in shadow. I'm hoping she's smiling.

"I bet this is what you do to impress all the girls." I can hear the smile in her voice.

"Just one," I reply, and though I'm joking with Riley, it's actually the truth. I've never thought of bringing Jo across to help out with the turtle monitoring, or anyone else for that matter.

"Oh, really?" Riley says, clearly not believing me.

"This is kind of my thing," I reply. "I haven't really shared it with anyone else."

"Well, I feel honoured that you're sharing whatever it is you're doing with me. It better be good."

I laugh. "You'll see."

When we get close to the beach on the island, I jump out of the canoe and push it onto the sand. Riley helps me pull it up out of the water so it doesn't go floating off on us while we're over on the other side. We grab our backpacks, and I lead Riley up into the dunes and onto the track to go meet Rosie. As we get to the edge of the trees, Riley takes my hand. "I can't see where I'm going," she says. I don't believe her, but I'll happily hold her hand for as long as she needs me to.

"Give it a bit of time and you'll get your night vision. The trick is to look above or beside the thing that you want to look at to see it properly."

"How do you know this stuff?" Riley asks as we weave through the bush.

"Grandad used to be in the army. He taught me when I was little."

"I don't think I ever met your grandad," Riley says. She's walking closer to me than she needs to but I don't mind.

"He lived in a nursing home in Townsville. He died when I was seven or eight."

"You never told me that," Riley says.

"I never thought to. It's not something you tell someone you only get to see for a few weeks over summer." I push up a low branch and hold it up for Riley to duck under.

"I guess not."

I can hear the waves breaking, which means we're getting close to the ocean side of the island. If Rosie is where she said she'd be, she should be about a hundred metres up the beach from where we'll come out on the track. We emerge from the trees and out onto the top of the dune. I lead Riley down onto the harder packed sand so it's easier to walk and I look for Rosie's head torch. The moon is brighter on this side of the island now that there are no trees to block it out.

"You still haven't told me what we're doing," Riley says.

I squeeze her hand. "You'll see. You'll love it, I promise." I scan the beach, resisting the urge to turn on my head torch, when I spot the feint glow of Rosie's torch just up ahead. I point it out to Riley so she knows where I'm taking her. "When we get up there, you can decide whether you just want to watch or want to help us out. It's totally up to you."

"There are other people on this date?"

I stop. "Who said anything about a date?"

Now that Riley's so close to me, I can see the expression on her face. She's got a cheeky one-sided grin and before I can say anything she leans in and kisses me. When she pulls away, I say, "Okay. You win. It's a date."

She laughs. "Let's get started then." She pulls me toward Rosie's light. I can't wait til she sees what's up there.

As we approach Rosie and the others, I can see there's already a turtle up on the dune. Sand is flicking out from behind her, so she must have just started.

"Oh my God," Riley whispers. "That's a turtle."

Rosie turns around. "Hey, Brooks. Is this the friend you were telling me about?"

"Yeah. Rosie, this is Riley. It's her first time."

Rosie stands up and shakes Riley's hand. "Okay, so I'll read you the riot act then," Rosie whispers. She pulls Riley and me away from the turtle a bit. "She's just started digging her egg chamber so you need to stay behind her. Once she starts laying eggs, that's when we can take measurements and check her tags and if she hasn't got any, we give her some. We'll also check for and record any damage. After she's done, we'll count her eggs and put in a nest tape recording all the details and then we're done. Once we mark the location, we head off and wait for the next one to come in. Are you going to help us out tonight, Riley, or just watch?"

"I think I'll just watch this one, if that's okay."

"Sure thing. When you're ready come on over and we'll get started." Rosie pats my arm as she passes and heads back to the others.

Riley grabs my hands and shakes them. "Oh my God this is so cool!"

"I know, right? Are you ready to see the real action?"

Riley nods and I take her hand and lead her back to where the turtle is now starting to lay her eggs. We stand around at the back of the turtle and when she starts laying, I point it out to Riley and encourage her to get closer so she can see. Rosie and Eric, the other volunteer, have their head torches on now so they can see what they're doing, so when Riley turns and looks at me, I can see the excitement on her face.

"This is really happening," she says.

I nod and smile. She turns and watches the turtle laying the eggs again and then when Rosie needs to get around to the back, Riley comes and stands beside me. "Cool, huh?" I say.

"Hell yes," Riley replies. It takes about half an hour for this turtle to lay her eggs and start covering the chamber back over. Once she's done, Riley and I follow behind her and watch her as she pulls herself back down to the water and disappears.

"What happens now?" Riley asks as we head back up to the dune.

"We count the eggs," I reply.

By the time we get back up, Rosie and Eric have started pulling the eggs from out of the chamber. Rosie hands one of the eggs to Riley, but she's reluctant to take it. "It's okay," Rosie reassures her. "They're pretty tough. Just don't drop it."

Riley cradles the egg, turning it over slowly in her hands. "There's a baby turtle in there?" she asks, looking up at me, amazement on her face.

I laugh. "Not yet. It's just like any other egg. The babies will grow inside over a couple of months."

Riley hands the egg back to Rosie, who places it gently on the sand beside the others. "So how long before they hatch?" Riley asks.

"Depends on the temperature of the nest and the weather," I reply. "Usually about eight weeks."

I can see Riley doing a quick calculation in her head. "So this one would probably be hatching in January or February then?"

"That'll be about right," Rosie says.

"Can I come back and see them hatch?" Riley asks.

"Of course you can," I reply. Riley squeezes my hand and smiles. We watch as Eric puts the eggs back in the chamber and as he starts covering them back over, Rosie's radio crackles to life.

"Looks like we've got another one just up the beach," she says.

As we follow Rosie and the volunteers over to the next turtle, Riley kisses me on the cheek.

"What's that for?" I ask.

"For sharing this with me," Riley says.

"You're welcome." I'm glad I brought her across, and I'm really glad she's as excited by this as I am.

After being on the island for almost four hours and having just seen off our third turtle for the night, it's no surprise that Riley's starting to fade really fast. I pull Rosie aside. "I'm going to head home. Riley looks like she's asleep on her feet."

"Okay. Thanks for helping out. I hope Riley enjoyed it."

"I'm pretty sure she did. Let me know if you need me tomorrow night."

"I've got a couple of students coming down from Townsville tomorrow so we should be right, but I'll let you know."

"Thanks."

"You know you're always welcome any time though."

"I know."

I watch as Rosie heads off up the beach to meet the others. We haven't spotted any other turtles coming in so they'll probably take a break now and get all their data put into Rosie's laptop. I pull on my backpack and take Riley's hand. "Ready to head home?"

She nods tiredly, and we head back down the beach to find the path back to the other side of the island.

Twenty-three

Riley

I can't believe I got to help out with nesting turtles. It was so amazing! I've never experienced anything like it before. I mean, I went to the aquarium at school a couple of years ago and got to hold an octopus and some star fish, but that was nothing compared to getting to touch real, live turtle eggs and watch them being laid by a real live turtle. And even though it's late, and I really need some sleep, I don't want the night to end, because the best part, hands down, has been spending time with Brooks.

I never really knew she was into conservation stuff before tonight. I realise now why she's so worried about Dad's development. I make a mental note to talk to him tomorrow, I mean today, about it (I think it's after midnight so it must be the next morning, right?).

"So," Brooks says. "Did you have a good night?"

"Oh my God, are you kidding? It was amazing."

Brooks drops my hand and puts her arm around my shoulder and pulls me in. "I'm glad."

I put my arm around her waist. It feels so good to be with her. "How long have you been helping Rosie out?"

"The last two years."

"And the turtles have been nesting on here for how long?"

"We're not sure. Rosie did some digging and found out that they used to nest here a long time ago, but she thinks that all the development on the mainland might have put them off until a few years ago."

"Why would that matter?"

"Something about the way they navigate," Brooks says. "The bright lights from Roper's used to throw them off, or so Rosie thinks, and since the council changed them to orange lights and got rid of a lot of them off the esplanade, the turtles seem to have come back."

I consider that for a moment and then a thought occurs to me. "Is that why you don't like Dad's development? Because of the turtles?"

"Yeah, mostly. But he had to do an Environmental Impact Statement, and part of it was how he'd protect the turtles during construction and afterwards when people start staying on here."

"So will the turtles be protected then?"

Brooks doesn't answer straight away. Finally she says, "Rosie seems to be happy with the EIS, so it must be okay."

We come to the end of the track and step out onto the dune and down onto the beach. Brooks turns on her head torch and looks around for the canoe.

"Oh shit," she says. She drops my hand and looks around frantically, the light from her head torch flicking around wildly.

"What's wrong?"

"The canoe. It's not here." She turns her head to the water and scans. "Shit. I can't see it."

I turn my head torch on and search around the dunes. "Are you sure we're in the right place?"

"I'm positive. I know this place like the back of my hand."

She walks up the beach a bit and then calls me. "Come look at this."

I stand beside her. "What am I looking at?"

"There," she says, pointing to what looks like drag marks. "Someone's freaking stolen the canoe. Shit!"

She throws her head back, throwing a stream of light straight up into the air.

"Wait a minute. There's footprints. Look."

Brooks bends down and looks at them. "Let's go see where they lead."

"Shouldn't we just go back to Rosie? I mean, we can get back to the mainland with her."

"She's staying on the island for a couple of nights," Brooks replies. "And we don't have any camping gear." She takes off up the beach, following the footprints with the light from her head torch. I have no option but to follow her.

A few hundred metres up the beach the footprints turn and head into the dune. As I follow Brooks, I realise where we are. "This is where the development is," I say.

"How do you know that?" Brooks asks, breathless as she powers up the hill.

"I was over here with Dad and Jason this afternoon. Dad was showing us where the camp sites are going to be."

Brooks stops and turns, sucking in short breaths. "You came over with your dad?"

I shrug. "Yeah. He took the afternoon off and we paddle boarded over."

The corner of Brooks' mouth turns up, just a little. "You paddle boarded over here?"

"Yes I did."

"Look at you being all sporty and trying new things."

"Can we just go find your canoe so we can get back?"

Brooks laughs. "Yeah."

We head into the trees, and this time I lead the way. I pick my way around small trees and bushes until we come into the clearing where the equipment is being stored. The site is surrounded by low orange lights and now I know about the turtles, I know why the lights are orange instead of white.

"There it is," Brooks says. She's pointing to the site office where Dad showed us the plans today. The canoe is laying beside it. Brooks and I head straight for it. We're halfway there when there's snarling and growling coming from inside the office.

"That's a dog," Brooks says, stating the obvious.

The door flings open and a security guard comes out, his flashlight shining in our eyes, his German Shepherd looking like it wants to eat us.

"What are you kids doing here?" the guard asks. His hand is hovering over the gun on his belt.

"Getting our canoe," Brooks says, sounding a lot braver than I feel with that huge dog still growling on the end of its leash.

"You shouldn't be here," the guard replies.

"It's a free world, and the island's not off-limits," Brooks counters.

"It is until construction's finished."

"No it's not," I say. Brooks' defiance has given me the confidence to speak up. "I was here today with my dad, Scott Fisher. I know you know who that is, don't you?"

The guard looks thrown, just for a second. "Everyone knows Scott Fisher," he says. "And I wasn't here today, so I have no idea who you are."

"I'd be happy to call him so he can tell you who I am. Although I don't think he'd be happy to be woken up at this time in the morning, do you?"

The guard narrows his eyes. "What's in your backpacks?"

"None of your business," Brooks says. "Just let us get the canoe so we can go home."

"I can't let you go until I check your backpacks." He takes a step forward, his German Shepherd walking beside him. Brooks backs away and the guard says, "If you run, she'll catch you."

"You know she's not supposed to be on the island? She could kill the wildlife," Brooks says.

"She doesn't kill anything," the guard replies. "Unless she has to." He sneers, but Brooks doesn't back down.

"It's in the EIS. You guys aren't supposed to use guard dogs on here at all."

"I wouldn't know anything about that," the guard says. "I just do what I'm told." He's now standing right in front of us. His dog now sits quietly beside him, watching us. The guard holds out his hand. "Backpacks, ladies. As soon as I see there's nothing dangerous in there, you can take your canoe and go."

I take my backpack off and open it up.

"Riley, he can't make you do that. He's got no right."

"I just want to get home. Don't you?"

She sighs. "Fine." She flings her backpack off her back and opens the top. The guard peers inside them both, gives us what I guess he thinks is an evil eye and says, "Thank you. Was that so hard?"

Brooks grunts. He watches us as we go over to get the canoe. As we walk past him again, I say, "I'll be telling my dad about this."

He has the nerve to smile at me. "See you later," he says and waves to us as we head back to the beach.

Twenty-four

Brooks

By the time we got back to the mainland in the canoe and I walked Riley home and got home myself, it was well after two in the morning. I just couldn't get that guard dog out of my mind, so I got out the paperwork for the development that I'd gotten from Mum back when I was protesting and went through it all again. I must have fallen asleep in the middle of it all, because when Ben wakes me the next morning, (thank God, since I forgot to set my alarm), I have it spread out all over my bed.

"I'd ask you what you're studying for but I know you never did that at school," Ben says when I finally make it out to the kitchen. I drop down onto a stool at the breakfast bench and lay my head on my arms.

"You're so funny," I mumble. I know I only have half an hour to get ready for work, but I am so tired I can hardly move. My whole body feels like lead and my eyes feel like they're full of sand.

"How late did you get in?" Ben asks. He fills up the kettle and turns it on.

"Around two."

"Wow. That's late, even for you."

"The canoe got taken by some stupid security guard while we were helping Rosie."

"What security guard?"

"The one at the work site."

"Scott's employing security guards now?" Ben leans back on the bench and folds his arms.

"Yeah, well, he's got a lot of equipment over on the island, so I guess he doesn't want it stolen. That's not even the worst part," I say, sitting up and stretching.

"What's the worst part?" Ben asks.

"The security guard had a dog with him. Can you believe it? I'm sure there's something in the EIS or some other paperwork about protecting the turtles."

"So that's what all the paperwork is," Ben says.

"Yep."

"Did you find anything?"

"No." I sigh. "But I'm positive Mum said that if Scott hired security for the site there wouldn't be any dogs there because it was one of the things Rosie brought up, so I'll have to go see her to find out whether that's true."

"Your mum or Rosie?" Ben asks.

"Rosie," I reply. "There's no way I'm talking to Mum about it. We'd only end up in another argument."

"Fair enough," Ben says. "What time do you start work?" He pulls two coffee mugs from the mug tree and makes us both coffees.

I look up at the wall clock. "In about twenty minutes."

Ben pulls a face. "You look like death. Maybe you should take the day off?"

"Actually, that's not a bad idea. I could use the time off work to do some more research into the development paperwork."

"I meant so you could catch up on some sleep," Ben says, handing me my coffee.

"I'll do both." I smile at him as I sip on my coffee and he just shakes his head. He picks up the phone and dials.

"Hey, Reece. It's Ben. Brooks isn't feeling the best. Yeah. Girl stuff I think." He pulls a face and I laugh. "Yeah me too. A day off will do her good. She should be in tomorrow. See you." He hangs up.

"Girl stuff?" I ask. "God you're embarrassing."

"Hey, that's the only guaranteed way a guy won't ask any more questions."

"You're a shit."

"You're welcome." He grins and drinks his coffee.

When I wake up it's mid-afternoon. I check my phone for messages and discover that I have a message from Gloria asking if I'll do the take away deliveries again tonight and a text from Riley telling me how much she loved last night. I dial her number and roll over so the phone is between my head and the pillow. It takes a couple of rings before she answers and I can't help smiling at the sound of her voice.

"Hey," she says. "Finally out of bed?"

"How did you know I'd been sleeping?"

"I can hear it in your voice."

"Here I was thinking I was just sounding sexy."

Riley laughs. "Actually, I called into the surf shop and Reece told me you weren't feeling well. I figured that meant you were tired after last night."

"Oh, shit. You didn't tell him we were late home, did you?"

"No," Riley replies. "Why?"

"Nothing. If he thinks I pulled a sickie he might drop my hours, that's all."

"Oh."

"It's no big deal," I say, trying to reassure her. "I had a great time last night."

"Me too," Riley replies. I close my eyes so I can concentrate on her voice better. When she speaks, she sounds like she's right beside me. It sends chills up my spine. "Hey, that reminds me. I left a note for Dad about the dog on the island. Hopefully I can catch him today to tell him about it."

I sit up, the spell broken at the memory of last night and thinking about the damage that dog could have done if we hadn't have found out about it. When I don't reply, Riley says, "Are you still there?"

"Yeah. I'm here."

"Everything okay?"

"Yeah. Why?"

"You're not saying much," Riley says.

"That's because I just like listening to the sound of your voice."

Riley giggles. "Oh my God, that's so corny."

"It is, isn't it?"

Riley doesn't reply. Instead, I hear her take a breath and let it out slowly. "Now you just sound like one of those heavy breathers," I joke. Riley snorts.

"So, what are you doing later?" I ask.

"Going through some more of Mum's boxes," Riley replies.

"Still?"

"Yeah." Riley must be moving around, because her voice is a little muffled. "Jason's offered to help, so that'll be good."

"Does that mean you're busy tonight then?" I ask.

Riley must get that it's a loaded question because she replies playfully, "Unless I get a better offer."

"Is helping with the deliveries a better offer?"

"Anything with you is a better offer," Riley replies, making my skin tingle.

"I'll swing by around six to pick you up then."

"It's a date," Riley says.

After she hangs up, I lay back on my bed, my arms behind my head and close my eyes. I used to love spending time with Riley over the summer, but now we're older, and we're reconnecting in ways I could never have imagined, the time I spend with her is that much better.

Twenty-five

Riley

Over the next few days, and with Julie's and Jason's help, I go through the rest of the boxes. Julie insists on keeping the boxes I want to give to charity stored in the garage for a few more months, just in case I change my mind. I doubt I will but it's nice of Julie to be concerned.

I've kept everything I want to keep, which is basically my old school stuff and the photo albums, and one of Mum's favourite scarves she wore when she started losing her hair. It still smells like her lavender body wash and it's become a bit of a ritual to smell it every night before I go to bed.

Brooks has had to work the rest of the week, and the only real time we've been able to spend together has been when we've done the take away deliveries for The Hut. Not that I'm complaining. After the last deliveries every night, Brooks and I have been laying on our backs on the picnic table at the back of the shop, looking up at the stars and talking about everything and nothing, just like we used to when we were kids. Although, you know, we never kissed each other when we were kids. We've had so much to catch up on, and by the time Saturday rolls around, I feel like the five years we didn't see each other never existed.

I'm just getting ready to jump in the pool at home when I get a phone call from Brooks.

"Riley," she whispers frantically. "Can you come to the surf shop? I need your help."

"Why are you whispering?" I whisper back.

"I'll explain when I see you. Can you come now?"

"Sure. Is everything okay?"

"I can't talk. See you soon."

Before I can say anything more, she hangs up.

When I get to the shop, Brooks rushes out and pulls me behind a rack of clothes and ducks down. "I need your help," she says.

"Who are we hiding from?" I ask.

"No-one. I just don't want Reece to see us together."

"Why not?"

"Because he needs to think you came in here by yourself."

"I'm confused."

Brooks pops her head back up over the rack, she looks around for a bit and then ducks back down. "Reece is with a lady over by the thongs. I need you to distract him away from her."

"What? Why? Brooks, what's going on?"

"Shh," Brooks says. She pushes her finger onto my lips and I have to resist the urge to bite it. "I need to get that lady."

"What's the matter with that lady?"

"That lady," Brooks says, "has enough clothing in her hands to put me ahead of Reece in sales for the first time this month."

Now it all makes sense. "So, let me get this straight. You want me to distract Reece so it leaves that lady open for you to take the sale?"

"Isn't that what I said?" Brooks asks. She doesn't wait for my answer. "We have to hurry up before he gets her to the counter."

I go to stand up but Brooks pulls me back down. "You can't come in with me," she says. "Reece will cotton on. Just wait a minute after I go back in, and then go straight over to Reece."

She goes to stand up but I pull her back down this time. "Wait a minute. Doesn't Reece know about us?"

"Irrelevant," Brooks says. "Reece still thinks he can get you."

Arrogant little— "Does he now?"

"Yeah," Brooks says. "He tried to bet me the other day that he could get you to go out with him."

"Oh, really? Does he not respect boundaries?"

"Nope," Brooks says, matter of fact. "So. Are you in?"

"Oh, I'm so in," I reply.

Brooks gives me a kiss on the cheek. "Don't forget to wait."

"Okay," I reply, and watch as she takes some clothes off the rack we're hiding behind and heads back inside. I wait for a bit before I stand up. I spot Reece near the back wall and make a bee-line for him. He glances up and I give him my most electric smile. When he smiles back, I know I've got him.

Twenty-six

Brooks

"I can't believe he fell for it," Riley laughs again. We're floating on pool mattresses in her pool, trying to beat the heat. There are more storms around judging by the stickiness in the air.

"I can," I reply. "He's a dick."

Riley pulls her sunglasses down on her nose. "Jealous, are we?"

I splash her and she splashes me back. She pulls off her sunglasses and gets all serious. "You're not jealous, are you?"

"No."

"Because," Riley continues, "I had to put up with a jealous ex- last year. It's not fun."

I totally ignore the jealous part because I don't want Riley to focus on it and instead pick up on the fact that she's dated someone else before me. "So I'm not your first?"

The corners of Riley's mouth twitch. "No," she says. I feel like the way she says it, she's challenging me to be upset about it, and the stupid fact is, I am. "I'm not your first, am I?" she asks.

"No."

She stretches her hand out toward me and I scrabble to grab her fingers with mine. We pull our pool lounges closer and Riley says, "So we both had practice runs."

"I guess."

Riley leans across and kisses me and as I lean into her, the mattresses flip out from under us and we plunge into the water. We swim over to the edge of the pool and look at each other, laughing.

"I almost forgot," Riley says. "I finally got a chance to talk to Dad about the security guard. He said he'd sort it out."

"Really?"

"Yeah. He was actually quite angry about it."

"Thanks," I reply.

"No worries," Riley says. She wraps her arms around me and kisses me. Man she's a good kisser.

Someone clears their throat behind us. We look up to see Julie standing by the pool gate. "Riley, your father wants to see you at his office. He's got something he wants to show you." I'm guessing that since she didn't say 'Hi Brooks' or 'Sorry to interrupt' that she's not happy to have busted Riley and I kissing in her pool.

I pull myself up onto the pool deck. "I should get going anyway." Riley follows me up via the steps. I quickly wipe myself down and pull on my shorts.

Riley kisses me on the cheek and says, "I'll call you later." She either hasn't picked up on Julie's coldness, or she just doesn't care.

Julie holds the pool gate open, and as I walk through, I can feel her disapproval as she watches me leave.

As I walk through the door at Uncle Pete's, my phone vibrates in my pocket. I smile. Riley must miss me already. I swipe the screen and it lights up with missed calls. They're all from Rosie. I wonder what's so important.

I check my voice mail, and on the first one, Rosie sounds upset and just asks me to call her back ASAP. In the second one, Rosie is frantic, and I can't make too much sense out of it at all. It's got something to do with the turtles, I can understand that much, but she gets cut off. I listen to the next one, which isn't Rosie at all, but one of the volunteers. "Hi, Brooks. This is Eric. Something's destroyed three of the turtle nests. Can you please call Rosie as soon as you get this? She needs your help."

I immediately call Rosie back. "Hey, Rosie. Sorry I missed your calls. I was at work most of the day. What's happened?"

"Brooks," she says, and I can tell from the waver in her voice that she's upset and about to start crying. "I don't know what happened. The nests are absolutely destroyed."

"Goannas?" I ask, though I'm pretty sure I know the answer already.

She takes a breath. "No, we don't think so," she says. "There are paw prints on some of the wet sand near the high water mark. We surveyed for foxes a couple of months ago and we thought there were none. I don't understand it. Maybe we missed something on that last one."

I can feel my jaw clenching. "No. You didn't miss anything. It was a dog."

"A dog?" Rosie asks. "But, who would have a dog on the island?"

"I know exactly who it was," I reply. "I'll sort it out. You just go and see if you can protect the other nests and I'll see you later tonight."

"Okay. Thanks, Brooks. I'll see you later."

I'm fuming by the time I hang up the phone. I don't even bother to have a shower or get changed. I grab my scooter keys from the key tray in the hallway, and head straight to Scott Fisher's office.

Twenty-seven

Riley

Dad's receptionist, Trudy, sits behind a high desk where you can only just see the top of her head. There are a couple of uncomfortable chairs to sit on and the 3D plans of the glamping project are in the corner. I wonder what Dad wants to show me?

Julie never said anything to me about it after I got out of the pool. In fact, she never said anything at all to me, and I know it's because she disapproves of Brooks. I sent Brooks a text to apologise for Julie being rude, even though it's not my fault, but I still haven't heard back from her.

I'm thinking of sending her another one when the front door bursts open, and Brooks storms in. To say she looks angry is an understatement. I leap up off my seat and Trudy jumps up from behind her desk.

"You can't just barge in here like that," Trudy says.

Brooks ignores her. "Where's your dad?" she asks me. Her face is red and her jaw is clenching.

"He's in a meeting," I reply.

"I need to see him, right now," Brooks says.

"You can't," Trudy says. "You should leave." She's surprisingly calm. Maybe she's used to people barging in to Dad's office going off about his projects.

Brooks is defiant. "I'm not leaving until I see him."

I put my hand on Brooks' arm. "What's wrong?"

"That guard's dog destroyed the turtle nests."

"Oh no." I don't know what else to say.

"Your dad let this happen," Brooks says, pointing at me. "Your dad let those turtle nests get destroyed."

"Why is it his fault? He said he'd sort it out."

"He lied," Brooks replies.

"No," I say. "No, Dad said that the dog would be gone." Before I can say anything more, the door of Dad's office opens and Brooks' mum walks out. Their conversation trails off when they see Brooks.

"Brooks," her mum says. "What are you doing here?"

Brooks rounds on her. "I knew this would happen. I knew I couldn't trust you."

"About what?" Brooks' mum looks stricken.

Dad takes a step forward. "What's going on?"

"Your security guard's dog destroyed turtle nests last night. You said they wouldn't have dogs on the island. It was all bullshit, wasn't it?" Brooks goes to step towards Dad but I put my hand on her arm and she stands still. "You just have no intention of sticking to anything you say you're going to do, do you? What else are you hiding?"

Dad doesn't answer her. Instead he says, "Get out." It's low and menacing and makes the hairs on my neck stand on end. "Get out of my office before I call the police."

Brooks' mum walks over and takes Brooks' arm. "You won't get away with this," Brooks yells as her mum pulls her out of the office.

I turn to follow them out but Dad says, "Don't you go after her."

I turn to face him. "Why not? She's upset."

"Because," Dad says. "She's trouble, that's why."

"Because she's upset that a dog belonging to a security guard that you hired destroyed turtle eggs that she's passionate about protecting? That's why she's trouble?"

"I wouldn't put it past her and her bloody protest group to have done it themselves."

"How can you even think that?" I ask. "I was there, Dad. I watched the turtles come in and lay their eggs and I saw how important they are to Brooks. There's no way she'd deliberately destroy those nests."

"What, you don't think she'd destroy a couple of turtle eggs just to make me look bad?"

I'm horrified that Dad can even think that of Brooks. "It's not just a few eggs, Dad. There would've been hundreds of eggs destroyed."

"I can't help that," Dad says.

"You just don't care do you?"

"Riley—"

"No, Dad. All you care about is your stupid development and making money. You don't care about anything, or anyone, else, do you?"

"Wait a minute—"

All of a sudden, this changes from just being about Brooks and the turtles. It's everything. "You didn't care when she got diagnosed with cancer."

"Riley, that's not true."

"Isn't it? You could ditch a meeting to stop Jason from being expelled but you couldn't even call me back when I left you all those messages about Mum."

"What are you talking about?"

"I know all about it, Dad. Jason told me."

"Jason? I don't—"

"And you didn't even come to see her before she died," I cry, cutting him off. "She wanted to see you, and you couldn't even leave your stupid office to come and see her." Hot tears are streaming down my face now and Dad's not angry anymore, but I don't even care.

"Riley, it wasn't like that."

"You weren't there when she needed you. You weren't there when I needed you. And you don't even care now, when I'm telling you that this matters."

"Riley, that's not true." He steps towards me, his arms out, but I pull away.

"You know the only one who's asked me about Mum since I got here? Brooks! Brooks is the only one who cares enough to even ask me how I'm feeling." I can see the anger flash across his face. I turn to walk out the door.

"I don't want you to see her anymore, Riley," Dad warns.

I don't even turn around. "You can't tell me who I can and can't see."

"I'm your bloody father," he replies.

"You haven't been my father since you stopped letting me visit." I push open the door and run outside.

I try calling Brooks but she doesn't answer. When I get home, Jason and Damo are moving the last of the boxes out of the guest room and into the shed.

"Look out," Jason says when I almost run into him coming out of my room. "What's wrong?"

"I just had a major fight with Dad."

Jason shifts the box he's holding onto his hip. "Everything okay?"

"No." I squeeze my eyes shut against the tears that I do not want to come. "I haven't got time to explain anything. I need to find Brooks."

"Why? What's going on?"

"She's really angry about something and I need to find out if she's okay."

"Have you tried her phone?"

"She's not answering."

"Well, if you tell me what happened, I might know where she is," Jason says.

I take a breath to calm myself down. "A dog destroyed some turtle nests on the island and Riley had a major blow-up with Dad about it. He kicked her out of his office and then told me I couldn't see her anymore."

"Wow. That's massive."

"Yeah. So do you know where Brooks will be?"

He thinks about it for a bit. "Well, if she's pissed off with Scott about something to do with the development, she might be with her protest group."

"Protest group?"

"Yeah. She didn't tell you about that?"

"No. She didn't." No wonder her and Dad don't like each other.

"If she's anywhere, then she'll most likely be with them. Probably cooking up some way to get back at him." For some reason he smiles at that. I wonder why he thinks that's funny.

"So," I say, trying not to get impatient. "Where will the protest group be, if that's where she is?"

Jason dumps the box on the ground and grabs my arm. "I'll take you there," he says. "Come on."

Twenty-eight

Brooks

To say Jo was surprised to hear from me was an understatement, especially when I told her to contact everyone she could get a hold of to convene a special meeting. When I walk in to the lounge room at her place, I'm not surprised to feel the temperature drop in the room.

"What's she doing here?" Sam asks, obviously not caring about the fact that I can hear him.

"Just, hear her out," Jo says.

"Why should we? She's the one who wanted out." Sam crosses his arms and looks away. It hurts me just a bit that he's angry with me, but I can't think about that right now.

"I need your help," I say.

Albie protests but Jo stops him. "Just listen to what Brooks has to say and then we can decide what we want to do."

I can see she's definitely in charge now and as much as that annoys me, I really do need their help. I think about what are the most important parts to tell them. The ones that will get them angry and wanting to do something. "A dog destroyed a heap of turtle eggs on the island last night. Hundreds of them probably. A dog that Scott Fisher allowed to be on there when he told Rosie straight to her face that his security wouldn't have dogs."

I can see I've got their attention. "If he lets that slip through, what else is he going to do? Ignore the part in the plans that says he can't build closer than fifty metres off the dunes? Or the one where he's not allowed to clear random trees?"

"What do you want us to do?" Sam asks.

"I'm not sure yet. That's why I came to you. I thought we could come up with something that would really show him that we're not just a bunch of kids making trouble."

"We could blockade the barge and stop more machinery getting across," someone suggests.

"That will just slow them down and won't really make any difference," Jo says.

"What difference does it make? Scott will be so busy with the Minister on Monday he probably won't even notice," Albie says from where he's standing in the back.

Jo and I both look at each other and it seems by the smile she gives me, the exact same thought has just occurred to us both.

"We're going to take this to the next level," Jo says. "We're going to disrupt the Minister's visit."

"How?" Albie asks.

"We're going to get across to the island and chain ourselves to the machinery," I say.

"I love it," Sam says. "Only one problem. I reckon Scott will have ramped up his security ready for the Minister, so how do we get in to the site without anyone noticing?"

"And how do we not get arrested," someone else asks. "My parents would kill me if I get arrested." There's a murmur of agreement around the room.

"Yeah," someone else says. "I don't want to do anything illegal."

"Like sabotaging the barge wasn't illegal?" Jo asks.

"Are you going to be doing it with us, Brooks?" Albie asks. "Because you've been noticeably absent the last couple of protests. How do we know that you won't organise all of this and then let us do it and end up in the lock up?"

I don't have time to argue with them anymore. I just want to make Scott Fisher pay, and if I have to do that by myself, then I will. I take a deep breath and let it out slowly before I answer. "You know, what? I don't care if you don't want to help. You lot have gone on and on over the last few months about making a difference and standing up for what's right. Now you get the chance to do something more than just sabotage a barge or stand out the front of an office with signs and you don't want to do it? Well, fuck you guys. I'll do it myself." I turn to leave and walk straight into Riley.

"Whatever it is you're planning," she says, "I'm in."

After the meeting, Riley and I are standing out the front of Jo's house, and she tells me about her dad saying she couldn't see me anymore and I feel really bad about dragging her into the middle of our fight. "It's okay if you don't want to do this," I say. "I mean, it might take a few months to calm down and then we can maybe sneak a few late night visits in or something when the dust settles."

Riley takes my hand. "This is important to you, so it's important to me. Besides, I just don't think Dad gets what you're saying. Maybe if I protest with you he might pay more attention."

"So what are you going to do now?" I ask. "He's going to try to keep you at home. He might even change the locks on the guest house so you can't get out."

Riley laughs. "He's not that bad. He's just angry, that's all. Besides, I don't think I want to go home yet. I don't have a clue what I'd say to him."

Before I can even think about what I'm doing, I say, "You can stay at my place. We have to get up early on Monday morning anyway to get across to the island, so it would be easier for us to leave from my place rather than you trying to sneak out without your dad or Julie seeing you."

"That's a great idea," Riley says, smiling. "I'll have to see if Jason can bring me some clothes though. Somehow I don't think a sun dress would be appropriate attire for chaining myself to a tree."

I laugh and squeeze her hand. Jo comes outside, and I can see her eyes drift down to my hand holding Riley's but she doesn't say anything. "So we're all organised?" she asks.

"Yeah. We're just about to head off actually."

"Okay. Well," she says, looking just a little uncomfortable. "I guess I'll see you Monday morning then."

"I guess so." I hand Riley the spare helmet and she jumps onto the scooter behind me. "See you on Monday." As I drive off, I glance in the side mirror. Jo's still standing in the driveway watching us. I feel a twinge of sadness for her, but then Riley's arms wrap around me and I feel her rest her head on my back and I forget all about Jo.

Twenty-nine

Riley

On Sunday morning, Jason drops a bag of clothes off for me at Brooks' place, and I'm surprised he's even packed my toiletries. I love how he's not even embarrassed to go through my things. When he hands me the bag he says, "Just so you know, the cleaner comes tomorrow and she's pretty thorough. So if there's anything you don't want her to touch, I can let her know."

"Thanks." I take the backpack and toss it over my shoulder. "Can you just put the wooden box on my bedside table in a drawer? I don't want it to get broken."

"I can do that," Jason says. "Anything else?"

"That's all. Thanks."

Jason pauses. "You know this will all blow over, right?"

"Yeah. I know."

Brooks comes back from the shed where she's organising things for the protest. "We should get started."

Jason turns to go. "I'll leave you guys to it."

"You're not going to help us out?" I ask.

Jason screws up his nose. "I really would, but I'm kind of on a good behaviour thing, so I've been trying to stay out of it." He walks a few steps and then he turns back. "I hope everything goes well. And I hope Scott doesn't come down too hard on you."

"Thanks," I say, and watch him ride away on his bike. I'm amazed that for someone I hardly knew before I moved up here, he's turning out to be a great little brother.

I follow Brooks inside and she leads me straight to her room. We sit on the bed, and Brooks starts pacing around making a list of things we're going to need. "Locks, chains, probably something to stop our wrists from getting sore. Food and water." She looks up. "Hey, can you pass me that notepad and pen?" She points to her bedside table.

As I pick up the notebook and pen, I knock an envelope onto the floor. When I pick it up, I notice the logo in the corner. It's from the high school. "What's this?" I ask.

Brooks takes the notebook and pen, and when she goes to take the envelope I pull it out of her reach. "Not important," she says. "Can I have it?"

"Is that about your expulsion?"

Brooks shrugs. "I don't know."

"What do you mean, you don't know?"

"I haven't opened it yet."

"Don't you want to know what you're doing next year?"

She folds her arms and looks at the floor.

I try a different tack. "You know, whatever's in this envelope could affect our relationship."

The corner of her mouth twitches. "How?"

"This envelope determines whether we get to spend every single day together at school. Or not, depending on what it says. I think I have a right to know."

She sits down on the end of the bed and stares at the envelope.

"I can open it, if you don't want to," I say. I drop the envelope on to my lap and Brooks sees her chance. She snatches it off me and leaps off the bed. "Come on, Brooks. You have to look at it sooner or later."

She doesn't answer.

"Don't you want to know whether I'll have to pine over you five days a week and only see you after three pm?"

Brooks snorts. "Fine. I'll look. But only because I know you'll annoy me until I do."

I smile. She takes a breath and unsticks the tab on the back of the envelope, and pulls out a white piece of paper. Her expression doesn't change at all as she reads, so I have no idea what the verdict is.

"Well?"

She tosses the letter onto the bed. I scoop it up and start reading. "Wait a minute," I say. "This says it's up to you. Is that right?" Brooks nods. "So, after all this, you get to choose whether you want to repeat or not?"

Brooks nods again, and then a smile slowly spreads across her face.

"What are you going to do?" I ask.

She raises her eyebrow. "What do you think?"

Before I can answer, Brooks' phone beeps. She glances at it and says, "Jo's just sent us a list of stuff we need. We should get down to the shed to see what we've got so we can let Jo know. Come on," she says, pulling me up off the bed. "We've got heaps of stuff to do before tomorrow."

A three-thirty wakeup isn't very nice, no matter who's doing the waking up. Brooks shakes me again. "Come on, Riles. We'll be late."

"Just five more minutes," I mumble, and roll back over.

Brooks grabs me and rolls me back towards her. "If you think I'm going to carry you, you have another thing coming."

I squeeze my eyes shut, and Brooks reaches under the sheet and jabs me in the side with her finger. I giggle and she jabs me again. She leans in, her mouth so close to my ear I can feel her warm breath. "Come on, sleepy head. We don't want to be late for the party."

"Okay, okay." I sit up and rub my eyes.

"I'll go make us some coffee to take with us while you get dressed. Meet me out in the kitchen when you're ready."

"Okay," I reply.

"And don't you go back to sleep," she warns.

I sit up in bed. "I'm up, okay?"

She kisses me on the cheek. "I'll see you in a minute."

I literally get dressed with my eyes closed I'm so tired and as I head out to the kitchen, I walk into the bedroom door frame. Brooks stifles a laugh. She's already half way through a bowl of cereal and she's got a bowl out ready for me.

"Make sure you have something to eat," she whispers. "We'll throw some snacks in for when we get over there, but we don't know how long we'll be chained up. I don't want you fainting on me."

I pull up a seat at the bench and pour myself a bowl of cereal. I don't even care what it is. I'll eat anything at this point. Brooks pours the milk. I guess she doesn't trust me to know when to stop. I don't blame her. I've never been a morning person.

"Are you always this slow in the morning?" Brooks asks.

"My brain doesn't function until after ten am," I reply. I shovel in a mouthful of cereal and I am fully aware that Brooks has ants in her pants, and wants me to hurry up. "Just go do whatever else you have to do and come get me when you're ready," I say. "I won't be any help until I wake up."

Brooks bounces off out the back door and in the time it takes me to finish my cereal and get my shoes on, she's pulled the scooter around to the front, packed both our backpacks, made up two flasks of coffee and is waiting for me by the front door. "Ready?" she asks.

"As I'll ever be," I reply.

Brooks opens the front door and then shuts it again. "Shit," she says. "Shit, shit, shit." She leans back against the door.

"What?" I ask.

"Freaking Donaldson's out there."

"What? Who's Donaldson?" I go to open the door but she grabs my hand.

"Local copper," Brooks replies. "If you open it he'll see us and then he'll know we're up to something."

"You don't think he saw you though?"

"I don't know."

I walk over to the front window and peer around the blinds. Across the road and two houses up is a police car.

"What's he doing out there?"

"Someone must have tipped him off. Damnit!" She throws herself onto the lounge. "How are we going to sneak out without him seeing us?"

I peer back around the blinds and try to come up with something. The car lights turn on. "Wait. Brooks, come look. I think he's leaving."

Brooks pulls back the blinds in time to see the police car pull out and take off. "Wonder where he's going in a hurry?" I ask.

Brooks grabs me by the arm and pulls me to the front door. "Who cares? We need to go right now."

I've had my eyes closed the entire ride, and I jolt awake when we get to the meeting point thanks to Brooks slamming on the brakes. I still feel half asleep, but I'm not nearly as tired as I was when I woke up earlier. I help Brooks get the canoe into the water, and jump in. If everything is going to plan, all up along the beach, people will be getting into canoes and kayaks and heading over to the island as well.

Even though he said he didn't want to be involved, Jason did some digging and confirmed what we thought - Scott had ramped up security at the site in preparation for the Minister's visit this morning. Having said that, there are only three guards on the island instead of just one, and theoretically, no dogs.

Brooks checks her watch and then pushes us off. As we glide silently across the water, I pull out one of the flasks and have a couple of sips of the coffee to try to wake myself up.

When we reach the island, we pull the canoe up onto the sand and head off to meet the others. Our group (me, Brooks, Sam, Albie and a couple of Rosie's volunteers) are all accounted for, so we move as close to the work site as we can without getting spotted and wait for the signal. Brooks checks her watch again. I can tell she's getting antsy.

It was a big call to use a few people as decoys, because we're hoping it distracts all of the guards and not just one of them. We do have a contingency though. We're all going to hit the site from different sides and at slightly different times, so that we can split their focus.

We're the second team to go in, so hopefully, the guards should all be so distracted by either the decoys in the water, or the first team to go in, which is Jo's team, that we should at least be able to get some of us chained up before they realise what's happening.

A few more minutes pass, and then all of a sudden, there's a commotion in the water. An air horn goes off, piercing the night and sure enough, a couple of torches flash through the site. Sam goes to jump up, but Brooks holds him back. "Not yet," she says. "Two more minutes." She turns to me. "Ready to go, Riles?"

I nod.

She looks down at her watch and counts down the seconds in a nervous whisper. "Five, four, three, two, one, go!"

Thirty

Brooks

The single best part so far is the confusion on the faces of the security guards. When dawn breaks, they're standing in front of us all, hands on their hips, with no idea what to do about us.

They've called it in on their radios, but they'll have to wait at least an hour before anyone can get across to the island on the barge because of the tide.

I called out for a head count earlier, and we've managed to get twenty of us chained to trees and machinery. Eight of us ended up locked in the site office after being caught and the guards haven't spotted them yet, but Sam and Albie are up in the trees, ready to unfurl a banner they made yesterday. Riley and I are chained to trees next to each other, and the rest of us are chained in a ring right around the site.

The mood among us is surprisingly upbeat. We decided against chants and slogans, mainly because we couldn't come up with anything good at short notice. I think the silence between us all speaks loads more than if we were yelling random stuff out, because really, no-one's even here to hear it yet except the guards.

"When do you think they'll get here?" Riley asks.

"Who knows. I doubt they'll bring the Minister over at all, but at least the media will get a sniff of something happening if they're stopped from coming over here."

"God, Dad's going to be so angry with me."

"You can't think about that, Riles. You helped come up with this idea, remember? No regrets now."

Riley smiles at me. "No regrets," she says. "Except one."

"What's that?"

"That our trees are too far apart for me to kiss you."

I laugh. "We have more important things to think about than kissing. But if you hold that thought, you might get to visit me in jail later."

Riley laughs and then leans her head against the tree. "What if they leave us here?"

"What do you mean?"

"I mean, what if Dad turns up and he goes 'Well, I don't want to cut those trees down anyway, so the girls can stay there and starve.' What if that happens?"

"You think way too much."

Riley does bring up a good point though. The absolute worst thing that could happen is if Scott totally ignores us and just decides to postpone everything and leave us here to teach us a lesson. There are storms forecast for tonight and tomorrow and it would be a pretty miserable time if we had to wait it out in the rain. Riley would freak out for sure, and I'm betting Sam would break and come down straight away.

I don't know how many others would just give up and beg to be cut free, because I doubt their level of commitment would extend to riding out a bit of thunder and lightning and a whole heap of rain. Before I can think any more about it, two of the guards rush off, leaving one to watch all of us.

"Something's happening," Riley says. She's closer to where the guards were than me and she cranes her neck to see if she can see anything. A few minutes later, Scott Fisher comes striding into view, Sergeant Donaldson beside him and a couple of other police officers behind them. Scott stops in the middle of the clearing and has a quick look around and when he spots Riley, his face sets in an angry grimace.

Following close behind the police is a camera crew. The guards try to muscle them out of the way but they manage to hold their ground. Sam and Albie see their moment and let go of the banner.

'Scott Fisher Turtle Killer' scrawled in bright red paint flutters in the morning breeze. The boys have also drawn what I'm guessing is supposed to be a green turtle with red blood coming out of it, with black crosses for eyes. It's pretty basic but it has the desired effect. I look back to Scott, whose face has drained of colour. He says something to Sergeant Donaldson, who in turn calls out, "Get them all out of here and take them all in to the station."

Riley turns to me and I can see she's a bit scared. She takes a deep breath. "This is it," she says.

I nod. "Everything's going to be fine, Riles. Trust me. They won't do anything to hurt you."

"You say that like you've done this before," Riley replies, smirking.

I smile back at her. "Just let them do their job. Don't fight them, okay?"

"That's it?" she asks. "Aren't we going to make a scene or anything?"

"We've made our point. That's all we wanted to do." A police officer bends down in front of me with bolt cutters and I have to stretch my head around him to see Riley, who's just been cut free and is being escorted away. "I'll see you down at the station," I call to her and she waves her hand to let me know she's heard me.

Thirty-one

Riley

A police officer leads me through an open office where people from the protest are starting to pile up, sitting on chairs and leaning against the walls. When I asked him what I was being charged with, he told me I wasn't being arrested. I was just being 'detained' until my father gets here. He takes me to a small office and opens the door. "Wait in there," he says. I step in and the officer shuts the door behind me. I turn to my right and there, sitting on a chair in the corner, is Jason.

"What are you doing here?" I ask. He jumps up and gives me a hug.

"No need to ask why you're here," he replies. "It's all over town."

"Really?"

"Yeah. From what I heard, Scott's really pissed. He had to delay the Minister in Townsville to sort out your protest."

"So is he going ahead with the ceremony then?"

Jason shrugs and looks at his feet. "I don't know. I've been here all morning too."

"Wait. Why have you been here?"

"Long story short, I rescued Damo from the water tower."

"You what? What was he doing up there?"

"He climbed up there and couldn't get back down," Jason says. "He gets these hare-brained ideas when he gets…" He pauses and looks up at the ceiling, searching for the right words. He looks back at me. "When he has too much red cordial," he finishes, emphasising 'red cordial' with air quotes. The way he looks at me, I get the feeling there's more to the story, but he's probably not going to tell me in a police station.

"Why wouldn't he get down?" I ask.

"He's scared of heights," Jason shrugs.

I laugh. "You're kidding? Is he okay?"

"Yeah. He's fine. His mum picked him up earlier."

"So what are you still doing here then?"

"Well, Scott was supposed to come and pick me up, but he got distracted for some reason." He raises one eyebrow. We both laugh.

The door opens and Julie comes in. She shuts the door behind her and she just stands there, looking at us both and not saying anything.

"Mum, I—"

Julie puts up her hand. "Save it, Jason. I don't want to hear it."

Again, she stands there and looks at us both. I can't stand the silence either. "Julie, I—"

"Don't want to hear it," Julie says, cutting me off too.

"Can't we explain?" Jason asks.

"I don't care what you have to say. Either of you."

I'm not entirely sure why she's just standing there and not saying anything or doing anything. She closes her eyes and takes a couple of deep breaths. "What's she doing?" I whisper to Jason.

"She's centring herself," Jason whispers back. "Some new meditation thing."

Julie takes one last deep breath and then opens her eyes. "Right," she says. "Let's go home." She turns and opens the door.

"Wait," I say. "That's it?"

"What did you expect? That you'd be thrown in jail?" Julie asks.

"I don't know," I reply.

"You think your father would really have you charged with anything?"

I think back to Saturday when I told him he wasn't my father. When I don't answer, Julie steps over to me and puts her hands on my shoulders. "Riley, your father is so angry with you right now, but he's still your father. And yours," she looks up at Jason. "I have no idea what he's going to do when I get you two home, but I do know that he wouldn't leave either of you sitting in a police station, just to punish you."

She opens the door, and Jason and I follow her out. As we head through the open office, I hear someone call my name. I look up to see Brooks being taken out towards the back door. I know she's being taken out to the cells because I came past them earlier. "Brooks!" I call back.

Julie takes my arm and pulls me to the front door. "Probably best if you don't see her for a few days," she says. I turn and watch as Brooks disappears behind the door.

Jason and I have both been under 'house arrest' (my father's words) for two days. When we got home from the police station, he was surprisingly calm. All he said was that he was extremely disappointed in me for aligning myself with a group whose sole purpose was to make his life a misery. Funny though, he never forbade me from seeing Brooks again, but by grounding me, he effectively stopped me from being able to see her anyway. And there's no way she would risk sneaking in to my house to try to see me. He also confiscated my phone, so I have no contact with the outside world until he decides I've suffered enough.

On the positive side, I now have a room inside the main house. Jason managed to convince Dad and Julie to let him use the guest house as a games room, so I get the room Jason was using as a media room. Jason helped me set my room up, convincing me to keep my single bed from my old place after he and Damo sanded it back and painted it for me, and Mum's ashes box now takes pride of place on the window sill, looking out over the garden at the side of the house.

I'm lying on my bed, reading one of Julie's trashy magazines, when Jason sticks his head around my door. "Hey. Scott wants to see you outside."

This must be important because apart from seeing Dad at dinner the last few days, neither of us have really made an effort to talk to each other. I know from the stilted dinner conversations that construction has started on the development and that the Minister came down the following day to do all the publicity stuff. So in reality, we only delayed Dad by a day. I haven't heard anything about Rosie or the turtles, and I'm hoping that Dad paid attention to the protest and actually did something about it. I guess I'll find out soon enough.

When I get to the garage, Dad's pulled the paddle boards out and is putting together the paddles.

"Hey, Riles," he says when he sees me. He doesn't sound angry, which makes me feel a little suspicious. Is he lulling me into a false sense of security? I don't remember ever being punished by Dad, so I'm not really sure what to expect.

"Hey, Dad."

"I thought we'd go out on the water for a bit. Are you up for it?"

I shrug. "I guess." If this is his way of punishing me further, he's totally missing the mark. We pick up the boards and head down to the beach. Dad doesn't say anything again until we're both in the water.

"Just so you know, we going over to the island. There's something I want to show you."

We paddle in silence for a while and then Dad says, "You know your mother was obsessed with the island?"

"No," I reply. "I didn't."

"We used to go over all the time before we were married."

"What did you do over there?" I ask.

"Bird watch. Swim in the ocean. Lay out under the stars at night." He turns to me and smiles. "Watch the turtles come in."

"You knew about the turtles?"

"They've been coming for years," Dad says. "Not many, years ago. More now. You're mother loved them."

I'm a little confused. "Then why would you develop the island?" I ask. "Won't that harm them?"

"Not if I can help it," Dad says. "Looking after the turtles was something your mum and I used to talk about a lot when we were kids."

When they were kids? Nothing is making any sense. "How long did you know Mum before you got married?" I ask.

Dad turns and looks at me, seemingly surprised by my question. "Why do you want to know that?"

I shrug. "You weren't married for very long. How long were you together for?"

Dad takes in a breath and lets it out slowly. "Well," he says. "I guess you could say we got together when we were fourteen, but we kind of grew up together."

"Fourteen? But that doesn't make sense."

"Why not?" Dad asks.

"Because, Mum told me you met at work."

Dad seems shocked. "She told you that?"

"Yeah. She told me she used to write your display home ads when you were starting out in your business."

"Yeah. She did do that, but that was way after we got together."

"Wow. Why would Mum lie about that?"

"I don't know," Dad says. "Your mother, she was a bit of a free spirit. Always in her own head. Maybe she thought it was easier for you to think we weren't together for very long." We paddle on in silence for a bit and then Dad says something that surprises me. "I should never have pressured her into marrying me."

"Why not? Didn't she love you?"

"Of course she did, Riles. She just wasn't ever going to be happy staying in Roper's. She wanted to get out and see the world."

"Why didn't you go with her?" I ask. It makes perfect sense to me that they should've left Roper's together. That Dad should've gone with her, and me, not stayed behind.

Dad stops paddling, kneels down on his board, and then as it glides to a stop he sits, his legs dangling over the side. I paddle up beside him and do the same. "Lots of reasons," Dad says. "It was a complicated situation, Riles. I guess, someone would've had to compromise and neither of us wanted the other to give up our dreams and hold the other back."

I can feel a lump forming in my throat. "But, you had me though, right? Why couldn't I keep you together?" Warm tears start rolling down my cheeks.

Dad looks up at me and his face softens. He reaches out and takes my hand. "Oh, Riles. If I could take back the last thirteen years, I would. Letting you go with your mother was one of the hardest things I've ever done, but there's no way I would have been able to give you the life she gave you."

I wipe the tears from my cheeks. "You don't know that."

"You're right," he says. "But it doesn't matter now. What's happened has happened and no matter how much we want to, we can't go backwards." He starts paddling and then he stands up. "Come on. Enough sad talk. I've got something that'll make you feel better."

I'm struggling to digest all of this new information. Part of me wants to just go home and not worry about whatever it is Dad wants to show me. I could turn around and head back to the mainland, but when I look behind me, I realise that it's too far away. Maybe Dad's right. Maybe it is easier to just keep going. I turn back toward the island and start paddling.

Dad and I skirt around the development site and head to the other side of the island. We wander up the beach until we spot Rosie's camp site. Rosie greets him like an old friend, which surprises me considering what's happened the last few days. "Is it here?" Dad asks, and Rosie points to a tree stump in a small clearing behind the dune. I follow Dad over and when we get there, he kneels down in the sand and places his hand on top of a blanket that appears to be covering something. I kneel down beside him.

"I wanted to keep this under wraps until I knew what was happening for sure. I wish I could have told you sooner, because it might have prevented the events that have occurred over the last few days." He rubs his chin. "The truth is, I've had this in the works for as long as the development has been but it's taken longer to get it finalised. I was going to reveal it with the Minister on Monday but, well, we all know how that turned out." He raises his eyebrows, but surprisingly, there's no hint of anger in his voice.

"Anyway, Riley, I did something that I hope you'll appreciate and that I hope makes you realise that, no matter what happened between me and your mother, I did still care about her, and you." He pulls back the blanket to reveal a long wooden sign. Carved into it is a name. It says:

Amy Fisher Nature Refuge

That's Mum's name. I feel tears welling up in my eyes again. "You named the island after her?"
Dad nods. "I did."
I swallow hard. "What about Julie?"
Dad half laughs. "Julie doesn't care for islands much. I promised her I'd name my first resort after her."
That makes me laugh. I trace the letters on the sign and suck in a breath. "She'd love this." Dad puts his arm around me and pulls me into a hug.

"She would, wouldn't she?" he says, and I hug him
back.

199

Thirty-two

Brooks

I haven't seen or heard from Riley in three days. Jo's been around once, just to let me know that C.R.A.G is disbanding, which is good news, and she just had to tell me that she's dating one of the researchers from Rosie's monitoring group. Apparently they met at the protest. I've got no idea why she felt the need to tell me, but whatever.

Dad's been around to tell me he's seeing a specialist about his knee, finally, and I've seen Mum once since Dad picked me up from the police station and that was only because I went home to help him in the yard. She said hello, and I could tell even that was an effort. At least we're back to not yelling at each other, which I suppose is something.

Ben's also made a point of paying me out for moping around the house over the last few days, and that's only because he's so head over heels for Nicki and can't wait to introduce her to Uncle Pete when he comes back at the end of January. At least someone's happy I guess. The only reason I've left the house now is because Gloria called me and asked me to come in to the Hut to taste test a new pizza for her. I know it's probably something Ben cooked up with her to get me out of my pyjamas, but it's free pizza, so I'm not complaining.

I'm sitting outside the Hut, surfing the net on my phone when a shadow falls across the table. I look up to see Riley standing there, smiling down at me. She's with Jason. I glance around but don't see Scott or Julie, so I reckon I might be safe enough to talk to them.

"Hey, Brooks," Riley says.

"Hey."

Riley sits down on the chair beside me. "How've you been?"

"Okay," I shrug. "Does your dad know you're here?"

"Yes," Riley replies. "He's lifted my and Jason's house arrest, but we have a new curfew of nine pm, which totally sucks." When I don't say anything in return, she says, "I have some news."

"About what?" I ask.

"The development," Riley replies. When I roll my eyes, she says, "It's good news, Brooks, I promise."

I look up at Jason, who nods. "Okay. What is it?"

"Dad's making part of the island a Nature Refuge," Riley says, like it's some great thing he's doing. "To protect the turtles."

"So this is his way of apologising for what that dog did? I don't buy it." I look back down at my phone. Riley takes my phone out of my hand and puts it on the table. She scoots her chair closer, so our knees are touching.

"He knew about the turtles before he even put the plans into council," Riley says.

"I knew it!"

"Let me finish," Riley says.

"Fine." I'm still not convinced about anything Scott Fisher has done, but I'll hear her out.

"Dad knew about the turtles and he was the one who pushed for funding for Rosie to do her monitoring over the last couple of years."

"I don't believe you."

"You don't have to, because it doesn't even matter. Dad decided that as part of the glamping development, he wanted to turn part of the island into a Nature Refuge, and get Rosie to run tours, showing people the turtles and teaching them about them."

"So it's a way of him making more money?"

Riley huffs. "You're not listening to me. I know you don't like Dad, but can't you just give him some credit for trying to do the right thing? Even if it's just for me?" She sits back in her chair, her arms folded.

I sigh. "Fine. So what does all that mean?"

"It means that Rosie can do her monitoring, and she can show people what happens when they nest, just like you showed me. And," she says, leaning in, "it's not even the best part."

"What's the best part?" I ask.

Riley puts both her hands on my knees and leans in close. "The refuge is going to be named after Mum."

She's so unbelievably happy that it's hard not to be happy for her. And I guess I should be happy too, because regardless of whether Scott had the refuge planned all along, or whether it's something he's decided to do to make himself look better after all the bad publicity he got after our protest, the main thing is that the turtles will be protected now. And Rosie gets to keep doing what she's doing.

I take Riley's hands in mine and I try my best to mirror her excitement. "I'm really happy for you, Riles."

"Thanks," she says. "So, I wanted to ask you something, and you can say no if you want, but I hope you don't."

She pauses, seemingly expecting a response, so I say, "Okay."

"We're going to have an official naming ceremony for the refuge this afternoon when the signs go up. It's just going to be Dad and Julie, and Jason and me and probably a few people from the government and the council. Dad wants to have something in the paper so there'll probably be some reporters and stuff there too."

"So just something small?" I tease.

Riley slaps at my leg and says, "Anyway, like I was saying, we're going to scatter some of Mum's ashes in the ocean, so it really feels like her place. I'd really love it if you could be there. Will you come?"

"Are you sure your dad will let me?"

"He doesn't have a choice."

"That doesn't exactly fill me with confidence, Riles."

She takes my hand in hers. "It'll be fine. I promise."

She smiles and I give in. "Fine. I'll be there."

Riley jumps off her chair and hugs me, and then she kisses me. I had no idea how much I missed her until right this minute. She pulls away and says, "I have to go meet Julie to put the finishing touches on the ceremony. Are you coming, Jason?"

"I might just hang out here for a bit if that's okay," Jason says. "I'll come over to the island with Brooks."

Riley bends down and kisses me on the cheek. "I'll see you both on the island then."

Jason and I both watch her as she walks away, holding her hat on her head to stop it from flying off in the wind. As soon as she's gone, Jason drops down into the chair beside me and says, "You have to help me stop the ceremony."

"Why?"

Jason picks at the edge of the table.

"Jason, what did you do?"

"It wasn't me. It was Damo. We were, just…" Jason drops his head and trails off. "Riley protects that box like it's something important and we just wanted to see what was inside it. That's all."

I can't believe he'd be so stupid. "That's all? That's all?! Are you kidding me? Of course it was something precious. It was her mother, Jason."

"I'm sorry," he says.

"What did you do with the ashes?"

Jason looks extremely uncomfortable. His leg starts bouncing up and down and he starts fiddling with a napkin.

I snatch the napkin away from him. "What. Did you do. With the ashes?"

"They went all over the floor and Damo panicked because she was coming and we didn't want to get caught so we swept them under the mat and then when we came back the next day to pick them up, Flora had been and I think they're in the vacuum cleaner." Jason says it so fast it all comes out as one word, but I get the most important part, which is that Riley's mum's ashes no longer exist.

I close my eyes and take a deep breath, telling myself to stay calm. Losing my shit at him isn't going to help, and my biggest concern is how Riley's going to react when she discovers the ashes are gone.

"What are we going to do?" Jason whines.

"You are going to stop hanging around with Damo," I say. Jason opens his mouth to protest but I shut him up by raising my hand. "He gets you into so much trouble it's not funny, and if you think almost getting arrested for climbing up the water tower was bad enough, you have no idea what it's going to be like dealing with Riley if she finds out that Flora sucked up the remains of her mother in a vacuum cleaner."

"I didn't get arrested," he says. "And besides, I didn't do it for Damo."

"I don't care why you did it. You could've gotten into a heap more trouble than you did."

"I did it for you," Jason says.

"You what?"

Jason runs his hand through his hair and sighs. "I found out about the protest you were planning on the island."

"So?"

"So," Jason says, like it should be self-evident what he's talking about. "I heard Dad talking to Donaldson after you had that fight with him at his office. He figured you'd be up to something. Anyway, Damo and I decided we'd distract the coppers so they wouldn't pay attention to what you guys were up to."

I can't believe what I'm hearing. "You deliberately risked your life so C.R.A.G could do our last protest?"

Jason nods. I'm not sure whether to be angry with him or thank him. I settle for neither and change the subject.

"I don't see what that has to do with you destroying Riley's mother's ashes."

Jason leans in a little. "Well, you kinda owe me."

I laugh at his audacity. "Mate, you are in no state to be calling in favours right now."

"Why not?"

"Because," I say, stabbing him in the chest with my finger, "you're the one in trouble here. Not me."

Jason slumps back in his chair and pouts. Damn it, I hate it when people pout at me.

"She's going to kill me," he says. One final attempt to play on my emotions.

"She's not going to kill you."

"Oh you know that do you?" Jason asks. He looks at me all sullen and then he says, in all seriousness, "She's going to kill me and put *my* ashes in that box and scatter them in the ocean."

I stifle a laugh. "She's not going to kill you because I'll help you out."

Jason brightens. "You will?"

"Of course I will."

"So you're not going to tell her then?"

"Me? No freaking way."

"What are we going to do then? She wants to do that ceremony thing and scatter the ashes. There won't be anything to scatter."

I lean back into my chair. "Just let me think about it."

Jo appears at the table with my pizza and says, "Sorry it took so long. Matt had to clean the ash and stuff out of the pizza ovens. He forgot to do it last night."

I thank Jo, and I look over at Jason and smile. "I've got an idea." I take my pizza, grab Jason by the arm and head around the back of the Hut.

A couple of hours later, I'm standing on the beach beside Riley as her dad makes a dedication speech. Mum's doing her best to ignore me as she stands off to the side. She'd be totally freaking out about my public display of affection with Riley, but I don't care anymore. Riley leans in and whispers, "Sorry you're still fighting with your mum."

"Small steps," I whisper back.

Riley squeezes my hand. "You'll sort it out."

"I know," I reply, even though I really don't know if Mum and I can sort out our differences. For now, we're being civil, at least for Dad's sake, and I guess that's a good enough start. I concentrate on what Scott Fisher is saying.

"And now to make it official, I'd like to ask my daughter, Riley, to come forward to scatter Amy's ashes." I let go of Riley's hand but she takes it again and pulls me with her. I glance up at her dad, but he doesn't say anything. As we pass, Scott, Julie and Jason follow us down to the water's edge. We all take a couple of steps into the water and Riley lets go of my hand so she can take the lid from the ashes box. She opens it up and peers inside. She turns to me and whispers, "It looks different to what I thought it would."

I resist the urge to smile. "I've never seen someone's ashes, so I wouldn't know."

"Me neither," she says. She reaches into the box, takes out a small handful, and then holds it out at arm's length. She lets it cascade through her fingers into the water, and as the last of it falls, she says, "For Mum."

She washes her hand off, puts the lid back on the box and wipes the tears from her cheeks. I put my arm around her shoulder and kiss her on the forehead. She sniffles. "Why do I feel like pizza all of a sudden?"

Jason coughs. I look at him and pull the 'don't say a word' face. I turn back to Riley. "I'll shout you one, in honour of your mum."

Two months later

"Come on," Dad says. "We don't want to miss it." I don't know whether he's excited to see the turtles, or because tonight's the night the film crew are here to record some footage of Rosie's eco-tour. Dad wanted to do a test run of the tour and the camp ground before the grand opening next weekend, and he's invited some people up to act as tourists to see what they think.

"I can't wait til you see who we got to do the promos," he says, as he strides up the beach to where Rosie's head torch is bobbing around. Jason grunts beside me. He was in bed asleep when the phone call came through, and he wasn't happy to be woken up. Brooks meets us half way up the beach. She's been on the island for a couple of hours, helping Rosie with the tour group from the glamping ground and getting everything ready.

"How's it all going?" I ask. I take her hand and she kisses me on the cheek.

"It's so painful waiting for something to happen," she says. "Everyone's getting a bit antsy, but it shouldn't be too long now."

"The tour group's okay?"

Brooks smiles. "There's lots of stopping for photos and stuff, and the camera guy keeps asking us to redo some shots, but apart from that it's been pretty good. The group's excited to be part of the promo."

"I just thought they were getting some footage of the turtles."

"I think these tourists will get us some extra publicity."

"Why?"

"Just wait and see when you get up here."

We reach the dune where Rosie and some other volunteers are explaining the process to the tourists. I'm a little curious as to what's so special about them but I can't see who they are thanks to the cameraman standing right by Rosie's shoulder. It also doesn't help that everyone's faces are in shadow. When Rosie sees Dad, she comes over and shakes his hand. "Glad you could make it, Scott," she says. "The first one is always the most exciting."

"Wouldn't have missed it," Dad replies. Rosie corrals us around in a circle beside the nest site and kneels down, shining a light on the sand. The cameraman kneels beside me and we all crane our necks over the top, trying to get a look. The sand seems to be shifting, just a bit, and within minutes the first turtle pokes its head through the sand. Brooks squeezes my hand and I lean into her. I can't believe that after seeing the eggs laid last year, now I'm watching the baby turtles emerging.

A couple more babies emerge from the sand, and then all of a sudden, the sand erupts in a flurry of activity as the hatchlings dig their way out and scurry down into a holding area the volunteers have set up.

I watch as Rosie picks up one of the babies and as she shows it to the tourists, I can hear the passion in her voice when she talks about them, telling them everything she knows. One of the tourists asks if she can take a photo and Rosie positions herself in front of them. The woman with the camera bosses the other tourists around, telling them where to stand and then finally takes a picture.

"Great. We'll get that up on instagram as soon as we have service," says the woman with the camera.

Dad would be pleased. The more publicity the better. I look over at him, his head bent over the holding pen, and when he looks up at me, he's grinning. "This is great, hey Riles?"

"Yeah," I reply. I haven't seen him this excited in a long time. I peer into the holding area at all the babies, clambering over each other, chasing the light from the head torches above them. The cameraman asks Rosie to repeat everything she just said, and she goes through it all again as the cameraman records her and asks questions.

One of the volunteers says that all the hatchlings have emerged, and as we wait for Rosie to do some final data entry on her tablet, I become aware that someone's standing beside me. Thinking it's Brooks, I say, "This is amazing."

"Epic," comes the male voice from beside me. I turn my head and in the light from the camera that's now pointing right at us, the guy with long dark hair smiles at me. "This is the best camping trip I've ever been on," he says. I smile back, and for some reason, I feel like I should know him. Before I can work it out, Rosie finishes with her tablet and tells us to stand clear of the enclosure.

"We'll follow them down to the water now," she says, "but they'll be attracted to the light, so no torches except for the ones from the volunteers." She lifts up the side of the holding area and the turtles take off, following the torch light from the volunteers down to the water. We follow behind them, stopping at the water's edge, watching them hit the water and disappear into the darkness, just like their mother did a few months ago.

Brooks stands behind me, her arms around my waist, her chin on my shoulder. I can feel her warm breath on my skin. "Have you worked out who the tourists are yet?" she asks.

"It's a bit hard to see in the dark," I reply. "Who are they?"

She brushes her lips across my neck. "Three's Company."

"No way!"

Brooks laughs. "Yes way."

"Holy shit. No wonder Dad was excited." I turn around to face her. "Oh my God. You've spent the whole afternoon with them."

"Yes, I have," Brooks says, sounding proud of herself.

"I can't believe you didn't tell me."

"I was sworn to secrecy. Besides, your Dad would have roasted me slowly over a bonfire if word had gotten out about Three's Company being in town."

I laugh. Brooks and Dad are starting to realise that they have more in common than they first thought, and even though he's beginning to like Brooks, he's started on the 'overprotective dad' routine because Brooks and I are dating. It's totally unnecessary but also pretty cool. "Are you going to introduce me?" I ask.

"I'd have to check with them and see if they want to meet you," Brooks says. I whack her playfully on the arm. "Ow! Of course you get to meet them. Your dad's organised for food and drinks up at the campground. Speaking of which, we should get going. I haven't eaten all afternoon." As we walk back up the beach, hand-in-hand, she asks, "Have you picked your subjects yet?"

"Have you?"

She bumps my shoulder with hers. "I thought I'd wait to see what my girlfriend picks."

"Why?"

"So I can spend my days perving on her from the back of the class."

I snort. "That's so bad."

"Yeah," she says. "It is." She stops walking and pulls me into her. Her arms wind around my waist and she kisses me, soft and slow. I have a feeling this year is going to be better than I thought.

Acknowledgements

There are always a lot of people involved in writing my books, from answering small questions, to digging me out of major plot holes to pushing me forward and giving me the motivation to keep going.

Huge thanks to Alison Bedford as always, for her English-teacher editing genius. I think you're the only other person who has read the book the same number of times as me and not gotten sick of it.

To Kylie Nothdurft for cafe kitchen advice and making me look like I knew what I was talking about when I've never worked in a professional kitchen before in my life.

To Jess "The Constable" Domrow, for explaining the difference between being 'detained' and being 'arrested' and never asking me why I ask the questions that I do. Also, your instinct for knowing exactly where I'm going with my series of totally random and extremely vague questions is amazing - I guess that's why you're the police officer.

To Ranger Shane O'Connor, thank you for making sure Rosie and her volunteers were doing the right thing with the turtle monitoring and knew what they were talking about.

To the inaugural members of my first First Readers Club, Naomi, Renay, Estefany and Anne - you guys rock!

To all my Beta readers, and everyone else too numerous to name who have had some small part in pushing me along the way, thank you! And to the readers who have taken these stories and their characters to heart and love them as much as I do, if not more, thank you too - you guys are the reason I write.

And finally, as always, to my wife, Teresa, whose unwavering faith and support propels me forward into each new bookish adventure.

Thank you!

I want to thank you for all your emails and messages regarding the GIRLS OF SUMMER series. I'm so glad you're enjoying reading them as much as I enjoy writing them.

The GIRLS OF SUMMER stories are written especially for and about you – first kisses, summer crushes, falling in love, for girls who love girls.

Please continue to share your story suggestions and comments by emailing me at selena@srsilcox.com. I love hearing from you and answer every email I get.

If you want to keep up to date with all the latest GIRLS OF SUMMER news, you can join my email list at www.srsilcox.com.

Thanks for reading!
— SR

About the Author

Selena "SR" Silcox started writing sweet romance stories for lesbian teens because she never got to read them when she was younger.

She quickly discovered it was a great way for her to relive her glory days from her childhood and make up for all the things she didn't do but wished she could have.

Like kiss cute girls and play professional cricket.

She currently writes the GIRLS OF SUMMER SERIES of sweet romances for lesbian teens, as well as the ALICE HENDERSON SERIES about girls who play cricket.

You can track her down on facebook, twitter and instagram, where she posts updates on her new house, sport, her dogs and trying to kick her procrastination habit.